# Orientation

# Orientation

and Other Stories

Daniel Orozco

ff Faber and Faber, Inc.
An affiliate of Farrar, Straus and Giroux
New York

Faber and Faber, Inc.
An affiliate of Farrar, Straus and Giroux
18 West 18th Street, New York 10011

Copyright © 2011 by Daniel Orozco
All rights reserved
Distributed in Canada by D&M Publishers, Inc.
Printed in the United States of America
First edition, 2011

These stories previously appeared, some in slightly different form, in the following publications: *Ecotone* ("Only Connect"), *Harper's Magazine* ("Officers Weep"), *McSweeney's* ("Somoza's Dream"), *Mid-American Review* ("Temporary Stories"), *The Seattle Review* ("Orientation"), *Story* ("Hunger Tales," "The Bridge"), *StoryQuarterly* ("Shakers"), and *Zoetrope: All-Story* ("I Run Every Day").

Library of Congress Cataloging-in-Publication Data
Orozco, Daniel, 1957–
  Orientation : and other stories / Daniel Orozco — 1st ed.
    p.   cm.
  ISBN 978-0-86547-853-4 (alk. paper)
  I. Title.

PS3615.R5883O75 2011
813'.6—dc22

2010038531

Designed by Jonathan D. Lippincott

www.fsgbooks.com

10  9  8  7  6  5  4  3  2  1

For Frances Mayes and Ed Mayes

# Contents

# Orientation

Those are the offices and these are the cubicles. That's my cubicle there, and this is your cubicle. This is your phone. Never answer your phone. Let the Voicemail System answer it. This is your Voicemail System Manual. There are no personal phone calls allowed. We do, however, allow for emergencies. If you must make an emergency phone call, ask your supervisor first. If you can't find your supervisor, ask Phillip Spiers, who sits over there. He'll check with Clarissa Nicks, who sits over there. If you make an emergency phone call without asking, you may be let go.

These are your in- and out-boxes. All the forms in your in-box must be logged in by the date shown in the upper-left-hand corner, initialed by you in the upper-right-hand corner, and distributed to the Processing Analyst whose name is numerically coded in the lower-left-hand corner. The lower-right-hand corner is left blank. Here's your Processing Analyst Numerical

Code Index. And here's your Forms Processing Procedures Manual.

You must pace your work. What do I mean? I'm glad you asked that. We pace our work according to the eight-hour workday. If you have twelve hours of work in your in-box, for example, you must compress that work into the eight-hour day. If you have one hour of work in your in-box, you must expand that work to fill the eight-hour day. That was a good question. Feel free to ask questions. Ask too many questions, however, and you may be let go.

That is our receptionist. She is a temp. We go through receptionists here. They quit with alarming frequency. Be polite and civil to the temps. Learn their names, and invite them to lunch occasionally. But don't get close to them, as it only makes it more difficult when they leave. And they always leave. You can be sure of that.

The men's room is over there. The women's room is over there. John LaFountaine, who sits over there, uses the women's room occasionally. He says it is accidental. We know better, but we let it pass. John LaFountaine is harmless, his forays into the forbidden territory of the women's room simply a benign thrill, a faint blip on the dull, flat line of his life.

Russell Nash, who sits in the cubicle to your left, is in love with Amanda Pierce, who sits in the cubicle to your right. They ride the same bus together after work. For Amanda Pierce, it is just a tedious bus ride made less tedious by the idle nattering of Russell Nash. But for Russell Nash, it is the highlight of his day. It is the highlight of his life. Russell Nash has put on forty pounds and grows fatter with each passing month, nibbling on chips and cookies while peeking glumly over the partitions at Amanda Pierce and gorging himself at home on cold pizza and ice cream while watching adult videos on TV.

Amanda Pierce, in the cubicle to your right, has a six-year-old son named Jamie, who is autistic. Her cubicle is plastered from top to bottom with the boy's crayon artwork—sheet after sheet of precisely drawn concentric circles and ellipses, in black and yellow. She rotates them every other Friday. Be sure to comment on them. Amanda Pierce also has a husband, who is a lawyer. He subjects her to an escalating array of painful and humiliating sex games, to which Amanda Pierce reluctantly submits. She comes to work exhausted and freshly wounded each morning, wincing from the abrasions on her breasts, or the bruises on her abdomen, or the second-degree burns on the backs of her thighs.

But we're not supposed to know any of this. Do not let on. If you let on, you may be let go.

Amanda Pierce, who tolerates Russell Nash, is in love with Albert Bosch, whose office is over there. Albert Bosch, who only dimly registers Amanda Pierce's existence, has eyes only for Ellie Tapper, who sits over there. Ellie Tapper, who hates Albert Bosch, would walk through fire for Curtis Lance. But Curtis Lance hates Ellie Tapper. Isn't the world a funny place? Not in the ha-ha sense, of course.

Anika Bloom sits in that cubicle. Last year, while reviewing quarterly reports in a meeting with Barry Hacker, Anika Bloom's left palm began to bleed. She fell into a trance, stared into her hand, and told Barry Hacker when and how his wife would die. We laughed it off. She was, after all, a new employee. But Barry Hacker's wife is dead. So unless you want to know exactly when and how you'll die, never talk to Anika Bloom.

Colin Heavey sits in that cubicle over there. He was new once, just like you. We warned him about Anika Bloom. But at last year's Christmas Potluck he felt sorry for her when he saw that no one was talking to her. Colin Heavey brought her a drink. He hasn't been himself since. Colin Heavey is doomed. There's nothing he can do about it, and we are powerless to help him. Stay away from Colin Heavey. Never give any of your work to him. If he asks to do something, tell him you have to check with me. If he asks again, tell him I haven't gotten back to you.

This is the fire exit. There are several on this floor, and

they are marked accordingly. We have a Floor Evacuation Review every three months, and an Escape Route Quiz once a month. We have our Biannual Fire Drill twice a year, and our Annual Earthquake Drill once a year. These are precautions only. These things never happen.

For your information, we have a comprehensive health plan. Any catastrophic illness, any unforeseen tragedy, is completely covered. All dependents are completely covered. Larry Bagdikian, who sits over there, has six daughters. If anything were to happen to any of his girls, or to all of them, if all six were to simultaneously fall victim to illness or injury—stricken with a hideous degenerative muscle disease or some rare toxic blood disorder, sprayed with semiautomatic gunfire while on a class field trip, or attacked in their bunk beds by some prowling nocturnal lunatic—if any of this were to pass, Larry's girls would all be taken care of. Larry Bagdikian would not have to pay one dime. He would have nothing to worry about.

We also have a generous vacation and sick leave policy. We have an excellent disability insurance plan. We have a stable and profitable pension fund. We get group discounts for the symphony, and block seating at the ballpark. We get commuter ticket books for the bridge. We have direct deposit. We are all members of Costco.

This is our kitchenette. And this, this is our Mr. Coffee. We have a coffee pool into which we each pay two dollars a week for coffee, filters, sugar, and Coffee-mate. If you prefer Cremora or half-and-half to Coffee-mate, there is a special pool for three dollars a week. If you prefer Sweet'N Low to sugar, there is a special pool for two-fifty a week. We do not do decaf. You are allowed to join the coffee pool of your choice, but you are not allowed to touch the Mr. Coffee.

This is the microwave oven. You are allowed to *heat* food in the microwave oven. You are not, however, allowed to *cook* food in the microwave oven.

We get one hour for lunch. We also get one fifteen-minute

break in the morning and one fifteen-minute break in the afternoon. Always take your breaks. If you skip a break, it is gone forever. For your information, your break is a privilege, not a right. If you abuse the break policy, we are authorized to rescind your breaks. Lunch, however, is a right, not a privilege. If you abuse the lunch policy, our hands will be tied and we will be forced to look the other way. We will not enjoy that.

This is the refrigerator. You may put your lunch in it. Barry Hacker, who sits over there, steals food from this refrigerator. His petty theft is an outlet for his grief. Last New Year's Eve, while kissing his wife, a blood vessel burst in her brain. Barry Hacker's wife was two months pregnant at the time and lingered in a coma for half a year before she died. It was a tragic loss for Barry Hacker. He hasn't been himself since. Barry Hacker's wife was a beautiful woman. She was also completely covered. Barry Hacker did not have to pay one dime. But his dead wife haunts him. She haunts all of us. We have seen her, reflected in the monitors of our computers, moving past our cubicles. We have seen the dim shadow of her face in our photocopies. She pencils herself in in the receptionist's appointment book with the notation "To see Barry Hacker." She has left messages in the receptionist's Voicemail box, messages garbled by the electronic chirrups and buzzes in the phone line, her voice echoing from an immense distance within the ambient hum. But the voice is hers. And beneath the voice, beneath the tidal whoosh of static and hiss, the gurgling and crying of a baby can be heard.

In any case, if you bring a lunch, put a little something extra in the bag for Barry Hacker. We have four Barrys in this office. Isn't that a coincidence?

This is Matthew Payne's office. He is our Unit Manager, and his door is always closed. We have never seen him, and you will never see him. But he is there. You can be sure of that. He is all around us.

This is the Custodian's Closet. You have no business in the Custodian's Closet.

And this, this is our Supplies Cabinet. If you need supplies, see Curtis Lance. He will log you in on the Supplies Cabinet Authorization Log, then give you a Supplies Authorization Slip. Present your pink copy of the Supplies Authorization Slip to Ellie Tapper. She will log you in on the Supplies Cabinet Key Log, then give you the key. Because the Supplies Cabinet is located outside the Unit Manager's office, you must be very quiet. Gather your supplies quietly. The Supplies Cabinet is divided into four sections. Section One contains letterhead stationery, blank paper and envelopes, memo pads and notepads, and so on. Section Two contains pens and pencils and typewriter and printer ribbons, and the like. In Section Three we have erasers, correction fluids, transparent tapes, glue sticks, et cetera. And in Section Four we have paper clips and pushpins and scissors and razor blades. And here are the spare blades for the shredder. Do not touch the shredder, which is located over there. The shredder is of no concern to you.

Gwendolyn Stich sits in that office there. She is crazy about penguins and collects penguin knickknacks: penguin posters and coffee mugs and stationery, penguin stuffed animals, penguin jewelry, penguin sweaters and T-shirts and socks. She has a pair of penguin fuzzy slippers she wears when working late at the office. She has a tape cassette of penguin sounds, which she listens to for relaxation. Her favorite colors are black and white. She has personalized license plates that read PEN GWEN. Every morning, she passes through all the cubicles to wish each of us a *good* morning. She brings Danish on Wednesdays for Hump Day morning break, and doughnuts on Fridays for TGIF afternoon break. She organizes the Annual Christmas Potluck and is in charge of the Birthday List. Gwendolyn Stich's door is always open to all of us. She will always lend an ear and put in a good word for you; she will always give you a hand, or the shirt off her back, or a shoulder to cry on. Because her door is always open, she hides and cries in a stall in the women's room. And John LaFountaine—who, enthralled when a woman enters, sits quietly in his stall with his knees to his chest—John LaFountaine has heard her vomiting in there. We have come upon Gwendolyn Stich huddled in the stairwell, shivering in the updraft, sipping a Diet Mr. Pibb and hugging her knees. She does not let any of this interfere with her work. If it interfered with her work, she might have to be let go.

Kevin Howard sits in that cubicle over there. He is a serial killer, the one they call the Carpet Cutter, responsible for the mutilations across town. We're not supposed to know that, so do not let on. Don't worry. His compulsion inflicts itself on strangers only, and the routine established is elaborate and unwavering. The victim must be a white male, a young adult no older than thirty, heavyset, with dark hair and eyes, and the like. The victim must be chosen at random before sunset, from a public place; the victim is followed home and must put up a struggle; et cetera. The carnage inflicted is precise: the angle and direction of the incisions, the layering of skin and muscle tissue, the rearrangement of visceral organs, and so on. Kevin Howard does not let any of this interfere with his work. He is, in fact, our fastest typist. He types as if he were on fire. He has a secret crush on Gwendolyn Stich and leaves a red-foil-wrapped Hershey's Kiss on her desk every afternoon. But he hates Anika Bloom and keeps well away from her. In his presence, she has uncontrollable fits of shaking and trembling. Her left palm does not stop bleeding.

In any case, when Kevin Howard gets caught, act surprised. Say that he seemed like a nice person, a bit of a loner, perhaps, but always quiet and polite.

This is the photocopier room. And this, this is our view. It faces southwest. West is down there, toward the water. North is back there. Because we are on the seventeenth floor, we are afforded a magnificent view. Isn't it beautiful? It overlooks the park, where the tops of those trees are. You can see a segment of the bay between those two buildings over there. You can see the sun set in the gap between those two buildings over there.

You can see this building reflected in the glass panels of that building across the way. There. See? That's you, waving. And look there. There's Anika Bloom in the kitchenette, waving back.

Enjoy this view while photocopying. If you have problems with the photocopier, see Russell Nash. If you have any questions, ask your supervisor. If you can't find your supervisor, ask Phillip Spiers. He sits over there. He'll check with Clarissa Nicks. She sits over there. If you can't find them, feel free to ask me. That's my cubicle. I sit in there.

# The Bridge

It was tradition on the bridge for each member of the paint crew to get a nickname. It was tradition that the name be pulled out of the air, and not really mean anything. It was just what you go by at work. But Baby's name was different. Baby's name was a special case.

Union Hall had sent him up when W.C. retired last summer. Although he'd been working high steel a few years, Baby was young, about twenty-five, but looked younger. He was long and skinny, with wide hands that dangled by thin wrists from his too-short sleeves. He had a buzz-top haircut that made his ears stick out. His face got blotchy and pink in the sun. He was the youngest in Bulldog's crew by twenty years. His first day, when Bulldog brought him to the crew shack inside the south tower and introduced him around, you could see this boy sizing up the old-timers, calculating the age difference in his head and grinning about it. He tossed his gear into W.C.'s old locker and flopped on the bench next to it. He pulled out a Walkman and started fiddling with the earphones. And while the crew was getting down to first things first, discussing a nickname for him, he let out a phlegmy little snort and muttered, Well, geez, just don't call me Kid. Then he turned on his Walkman, opened his mouth, and shut his eyes. Bulldog and the crew regarded him for a moment, this skinny, openmouthed boy stretched out on W.C.'s bench, his big, booted feet bouncing fitfully to the tinny scratching of music coming from his ears. The painters then returned to the matter at hand. They would not call him Kid. They would not call him Sonny or Junior, either. They would go one better. With little discussion, they decided to veer from tradition just this once, and Baby's name was born.

Being new to bridge painting, Baby is still getting the hang of things, with his partner, Whale, telling him to check his harness, to yank on it at least a hundred times a day to make sure it's fast; to check that his boots are laced up, because there's no tripping allowed, not up here, the first step is a killer; and to always attach his safety line, to clip it onto *anything* and *everything*. Baby listens, but under duress, rolling his eyes and muttering, Yeah, yeah, yeah, I got it, I got it, which sets Whale off. But Bulldog and the rest of them tell him to take it easy. They are old hands at this, they remind him. They are cautious and patient men, and Baby's just young, that's all. He'll learn to slow down, as each of them learned; he'll learn to get used to the steady and deliberate pace of their work, what Bulldog calls the Art of Painting a Bridge: degreasing a section of steel first; sandblasting and inspecting for corrosion; and after the iron crew's done replacing the corroded plates or rivets or whatever, blasting again; sealing the steel with primer one, and primer two the next day; then top coat one the day after that, and top coat two the day after that.

•

Whale doesn't like working with Baby, but he's partnered with him. So the two of them are under the roadbed, up inside the latticework. They go from the joists down, moving east to west along a row of crossbeams on the San Francisco side of the south tower. Whale is blasting rust out of a tight spot behind a tie brace, and Baby moves in to spray primer one, when suddenly his paint gun sputters and dies. He yanks off his noise helmet, shouts at Whale over the wind, and unclips his safety line to go look for the kink in his paint hose. Pissed off, Whale yells, God-dammit, but it's muffled under his helmet. Baby clunks down the platform in his big spattered boots. His line trails behind him, the steel carabiner clip skittering along the platform grating.

He spots the trouble right away, at the east end, just over his head—a section of hose hung up between the power line and the scaffold cable. He reaches up, stands on his toes, and leans out a little, his hips high against the railing. He grasps the hose, snaps it once, twice, three times until it clears. And just as he's turning around to give Whale the thumbs-up, a woman appears before him, inches from his face. She passes into and out of his view in less than two seconds. But in Baby's memory, she would be a woman floating, suspended in the flat light and the gray, swirling mist.

The witnesses said she dived off the bridge headfirst. They said she was walking along when she suddenly dropped her book bag and scrambled onto the guardrail, balancing on the top rail for a moment, arms over her head, then bouncing once from bended knees and disappearing over the side. It happened so fast, according to one witness. It was a perfect dive, accord-ing to another.

But her trajectory was poor. Too close to the bridge, her foot smashed against a beam, spinning her around and pointing her feet and legs downward. She was looking at Baby as she went past him, apparently just as surprised to see him as he was to see her. She was looking into his face, into his eyes, her arms up-stretched, drawing him to her as she dropped away.

And wondering how you decide to remember what you remember, wondering why you retain the memory of one detail and not another, Baby would remember, running those two seconds over and over in his head, her hands reaching toward him, fingers splayed, and her left hand balling into a fist just before the fog swallowed her. He would remember a thick, dark green pullover sweater, and the rush of her fall bunching the green under her breasts, revealing a thin, pale waist and a fluttering white shirttail. He would remember bleached blue jeans with rips flapping at both knees, and basketball shoes—those red high-tops that kids wear—and the redness of them arcing around, her legs and torso following as she twisted at the hips and straightened out, knifing into the bed of fog below. But what he could not remember was her face. Although he got a good look at her—at one point just about nose to nose, no more than six inches away—it was not a clear, sustained image of her face that stayed with him, but a flashing one, shutter-clicking on and off, on and off in his head. He could not remember a single detail. Her eyes locked on his as she went past and down, and Baby could not—for the life of him, and however hard he tried—remember what color they were.

But he would remember hearing, in spite of the wind whistling in his ears, in spite of the roar of traffic, the locomotive clatter of tires over the expansion gaps in the roadbed above, in spite of the hysterical thunking of the air compressor in the machine shed directly over him—Baby would remember hearing, as she went past, a tiny sound, an *oof* or an *oops*, probably her reaction to her ankle shattering against the beam above less than a second before. It was a small, muted grunt, a sound of minor exertion, of a small effort completed, the kind of sound that Baby had associated—before today—with plopping a heavy bag of groceries on the kitchen table or getting up, woozy, after having squatted on his knees to zip up his boy's jacket.

•

Whale drops his gun and goes clomping down the platform after Baby, who stands frozen, leaning out and staring down, saying, Man oh man, man oh man oh man. He gets to him just as Baby's knees buckle and hooks his safety line first thing. He pulls him to his feet, pries his gloved fingers from around the railing, and walks him to the other end of the platform. He hangs on to Baby as he reels the scaffold back under the tower, too fast. The wet cables slip and squeal through their pulleys, and the platform jolts and shudders until it slams finally into the deck with a reassuring clang. He unhooks their safety lines—Baby's first, then his own—and reaches out to clip them onto the ladder. He grabs a fistful of Baby's harness, and eases him—limp and obedient—over the eighteen-inch gap between the scaffold gate and the ladder platform. He puts Baby's hands on the first rung. They brace themselves as they swing out, the gusts always meaner on the west side of the bridge. The shifting winds grab at their parkas and yank at their safety lines, the yellow cords billowing out in twin arcs, then whipping at their backs and legs. They go one rung at a time, turtling up the ladder in an intimate embrace—Whale on top of Baby, belly to back, his mouth warm in Baby's ear, whispering, Nice and easy, Baby, over and over. That's it, Baby, nice and easy, nice and easy. Halfway up, they can hear the Coast Guard cutter below them, its engines revving and churning as it goes past, following the current out to sea.

They knock off a little early. In the parking lot, Baby leans against his car, smoking another cigarette, telling Whale and Bulldog and Gomer that he's okay, that he'll be driving home in a minute, just let him finish his cigarette, all right? Whale looks over at Gomer, then takes Baby's car keys and drives him home. Gomer follows in his car and gives Whale a ride back to the lot.

•

Suiting up in the crew shack the next morning, they ask him how he's doing, did he get any sleep, and he says Yeah, he's okay. So they take this time, before morning shift starts, to talk about it a little bit, all of them needing to talk it out for a few minutes, each of them having encountered jumpers, with C.B. seeing two in one day—just hours apart—from his bosun's platform halfway up the north tower, first one speck, then another, going over the side and into the water, and C.B. not being able to do anything about it. And Whale taking hours to talk one out of it once, and her calling him a week later to thank him, then jumping a week after that. And Bulldog having rescued four different jumpers from up on the pedestrian walkway, but also losing three up there, one of them an old guy who stood shivering on the five-inch-wide ledge just outside the rail and seven feet below the walkway, shivering there all afternoon in his bathrobe and slippers, looking like he'd taken a wrong turn on a midnight run to the toilet; and after standing there thinking about it, changing his mind, and reaching through the guardrail for Bulldog's outstretched arm, and brushing the tips of Bulldog's fingers before losing his footing.

Nobody says anything. Then Bulldog slaps his thighs and stands up. But that's how it goes, he says, and he tells everybody to get a move on, it's time to paint a bridge.


At lunch, Baby is looking through the paper. He tells Gomer and C.B. and the rest of them how he hates the way they keep numbering jumpers. She was the 995th, and he wished they'd stop doing that. And when they're reeling in the scaffold for afternoon break, he turns to Whale and tells him—without Whale's asking—that the worst thing about it was that he was the last person, the last living human being she saw before she died, and he couldn't even remember what she looked like, and he didn't need that, he really didn't.

And that's when Baby loses his noise helmet. It slips out

from the crook of his arm, hits the scaffold railing, and lobs over the side. It being a clear day, they both follow the helmet all the way down, not saying anything, just leaning out and watching it, squinting their eyes from the sun reflecting off the surface of the bay, and hearing it fall, the cowl fluttering and snapping behind the headpiece, until the helmet hits with a loud, sharp crack, like a gunshot. Not the sound of something hitting water at all.

At break, Baby's pretty upset. But Bulldog tells him not to sweat it, the first helmet's free. Yeah, Red says, but after that it costs you, and Red should know, having lost three helmets in his nineteen years. But Baby can't shut up about it. He goes on about the sound it made when it hit the water, about how amazing it is that from 220 feet up you can single out one fucking sound. He's worked up now. His voice is cracking, his face is redder than usual. They all look at him, then at each other, and Bulldog sits him down while the rest of them go out to work. Baby tells him he's sorry about the helmet, he really is, and that it won't happen again. And that's when Bulldog tells him to go on home. Go home, he says, and kiss your wife. Take the rest of the day, Bulldog says, I'll clear it with the Bridge Captain, no sweat.


Everybody's suiting up for morning shift. It's a cold one today, with the only heat coming from the work lights strung across a low beam overhead. They climb quickly into long johns and wool shirts and sweaters and parkas. They drink their coffee, fingers of steam rising from open thermoses, curling up past the lights. They wolf down doughnuts that Red brought. Whale is picking through the box, looking for an old-fashioned glazed, and C.B. is complaining to Red why he never gets those frosted sprinkled ones anymore, when Baby, who hasn't said a word since coming back, asks nobody in particular if he could maybe get a new nickname.

The painters all look at each other. Tradition says you don't change the nickname of a painter on the bridge. You just never do that. But on the other hand, it seems important to the boy, and sometimes you have to accommodate the members of your crew because that's what keeps a paint crew together. They watch him sitting there, concentrating on re-lacing his boots, tying and untying them, saying, It's no big deal, really, it's just that I never liked the name you gave me, and I was just wondering.

So they take these few minutes before the morning shift to weigh this decision. Whale chews slowly on the last old-fashioned glazed. Bulldog pours himself another half cup, and C.B. and Red both sit hunched over, coiling and uncoiling safety line. Gomer tips his chair back, dances it on its rear legs, and stares up past the work lights. The boy clears his throat, then falls silent. He watches Gomer rocking back and forth. He follows his gaze upward. Squinting past the lights, peering into the dark, he listens to the gusts outside whistling through the tower above them.

*So they did eat, and were well filled: for he gave them their own desire . . .*
                                                        —*Psalm 78:29*

# Hunger Tales

S

he went grocery shopping three times a week, after aerobics class, stopping at a market that was on her route from the fitness center to her apartment. It was a tiny family-owned place, with a splintered wood floor and two checkout stands, dimly lit and narrow-aisled and very popular with urban professionals. They carried microbrews and power bars and arugula, plus all the staples. So when she needed bread, bananas, carrots, milk—the usual things—she stopped there.

But when she felt she deserved a treat, then a special trip—a cookie run—was in order. For such trips she preferred to go to the biggest supermarkets she could find, places that employed so many checkers and rotated them so frequently that she could never become a regular to any of them. She always went late at night, when there were fewer people. And she liked to make the rounds, to zero in on the cookie aisle by switchbacking up and down all the other aisles, from one end of the store to the other. She did not linger on the perimeters of a supermarket. Seafood and Meat, Bakery, Produce, Deli, Dairy—these areas did not sustain her interest at all. The aisles drew her, and specifically, a particular effect of her passage through them: with each turn she took, a gallery of foods unfolded before her, glutting her field of view in a visual engorgement that made her skin tingle and her innards twitch and pucker, a kind of pre-cookie jitters that never failed to arouse her in an unsettlingly erotic way. The cookies would be gone fifteen minutes after she got them home—sooner if she opened the package in the car and started in on them while driving. Afterward, she would lie groggy on the sofa in front of the TV, sugar levels plunging, euphoria slipping away, feeling bloated and guilty and alone until she nodded off to sleep.

One night she drove to her favorite spot, a twenty-four-hour mega-market located at a mall just past the airport. It was the newly opened flagship store of a regional chain. It had twenty-six aisles, an all-night pharmacy and café, a video store, and a lounge with sofas and reading lamps and a fireplace with imitation logs burning in it. She scooped up a handbasket just inside the automatic doors, skirted the lounge, and headed directly for aisle 1A. These could be long nights for her. She could browse for hours, reveling not just in the sheer quantity of products but in their ever-expanding variety: there were ice creams with chocolate-covered pretzels or fudge brownie chunks or *real* vanilla bean specks in them, and made with organic strawberries or kosher cream or nuts not grown in a rain forest; there were white, yellow, blue, and red corn tortilla chips, and brown-, black-, green-, and orange-colored pastas; there were breakfast cereals shaped like peanuts, like raspberries, like doughnuts and cinnamon rolls, like waffles, like tiny slices of French toast; there were fifteen kinds of pasta sauce, ten flavors of rice cakes, and a dozen different flavors of carbonated water; there were eight varieties of something as simple as mustard. She felt immersed in abundance, gliding along like a love-drunk paramour, idly tossing items into her handbasket: brown sugar from aisle 2A, a can of sliced peaches from 7B, a box of raisins from 9B. At the end of the evening she would return most of these selections to their shelves, retaining only one or two benign items as counterbalance to the cookies. She never bought just the cookies. Nobody, she felt, needed to know that much about her.

But tonight, something was wrong. Although it was well past midnight, the supermarket was crowded. She had to squeeze past double-parked carts and around clusters of chatty shoppers blocking her path. Other late-night browsers began to loiter annoyingly on the periphery of her own late-night browsing. They sidled up next to her, perusing the same shelves she was perusing, their hands reaching for the jam jar next to the jam jar she had her hand on. One fellow trailed her all the way down the cereal aisle—inadvertently, she was sure—but persistently enough to compel her to move on. And worse, there were employees everywhere. They were crawling all over the place in their clip-on bow ties and starched blue aprons with name tags on them, briskly restocking shelves, trucking out head-high pallets of more boxed goods and taking box cutters to them with the panache of sushi chefs. They kept asking her if she needed help finding anything, and she kept saying "*No*, thank you." She felt so rushed and prodded, so frustrated at losing the rhythm of the evening, that she curtailed her usual route. She skipped aisles 12 through 21 and headed directly for 22B, the bull's-eye of her desire's meandering arrow—Cookies and Crackers. Once there, she never varied in her selection—it was always either the Nabisco Chunky Chips Ahoy or the Keebler Chocolate Lovers' Chips Deluxe. Yet she liked to mull over this choice, to savor the pretense of having to decide between one cookie or the other from the panoply before her: Which of you comes home with me tonight?

But even here she was hampered. There were people in the aisle—a couple, a man and a woman standing not just at the cookie shelves, but planted right in front of the Nabisco-Keebler array. She stopped a few yards up from them and pretended to scan the cracker shelves, waiting for them to leave. They both had shoulder-length hair and wore stylish black trench coats that made them look long and lean. They were young—in their mid-twenties, she guessed—and very attractive. They were standing there, hands deep in their coat pockets, talking intently, not leaving. She went back to Dairy and exchanged her two percent cottage cheese for one percent, then to aisle 6A to put back the sliced peaches. She returned to 22B. They were still there, in the exact same spot, slouching comfortably and murmuring to each other in that enticing and arrogant way couples in public do, inviting our exclusion from their intimacy. See how *we* can hear each other, they seemed to be letting the rest of us know. See how what *we* share is just out of your range.

She walked stiffly past them and went down the adjacent aisle, Pastas and Grains. She stood at the shelves, blindly running her hand over the packages. She heard the man's voice rise in pitch, heard the woman laugh. What could she be laughing about, for Christ's sake? She listened to their low, muffled tones, the thrum of their voices languid and melodic. There was more laughter, until finally—finally!—she heard them moving away. She trailed along, paralleling their slow progress out of the aisle, when suddenly a blue-aproned employee appeared before her, a tall, boyish, rawboned man with a big smile and a receding hairline and a name tag that read BRAD IS HAPPY TO SERVE YOU! He asked if he could help her find anything tonight. *"No!"* she thundered, rushing past him only to barrel into the cookie aisle couple. She muttered an apology as she plowed between them, then took the turn into aisle 22B.

It was empty, at last. "Yes," she said, reaching the cookie shelves. And she was standing before them for just a few seconds— she had hardly taken them all in, still adjusting her position so that they would fill as much of her peripheral vision as possible— she had *just* gotten to the cookie shelves when a woman moving past the end of the aisle turned to look at her. She, too, wore running shoes and tights and a big, fleecy sweater. Her dark hair was pulled taut into a ponytail that highlighted an unblemished face. The woman's gaze moved idly over her, then to the cookies she'd been looking at, then back to her. And just before gliding out of view beyond the end-aisle display, the woman's impassive face registered a barely discernible smile. It was a small and intimate grin, the tiniest check mark of a smile, but in its tininess was laden a knowledge of her so large—so complete an understanding of her evenings alone in these supermarkets, her enthrallment before these cookies, and the aftermath of it all—that she fled. She ran. She raced out the other end of the aisle and along the back of the market, loping past Seafood and Meat to the far end of the store, to take refuge in Produce. She paced among the bins, between homely mounds of polished fruit, breathing heavily, her eyes stinging, acutely aware of her own ridiculousness. She didn't know whether to laugh or cry. "Stupid!" she hissed. "Stupid, stupid!" Yet back and forth she went, hemmed in by her desolate longing, blinking and pacing amid the shine and sparkle of mirrors and the reflected abundance of freshly misted vegetables.

II.

It was late afternoon and he was watching TV. He was sitting on a love seat that had one arm sawed off to accommodate his girth. The rear legs were raised on four-by-sixes, so that he was positioned on a forward incline. A rope was within reach, one end looped loosely around a nearby floor lamp, the other bound to an anchor bolt drilled into a ceiling joist. He used this rope to pull himself out of the seat when he had to go to the bathroom, an operation that could take forty-five minutes—hauling himself up, teetering toward the wall and groping along it for balance, squeezing through the doorframe (the door had been removed long ago), shitting or pissing into the tarp-lined tub, then moving carefully back toward his seat, sliding along the tracks sanded into the wood floor by his thickly callused feet. He did not want to fall. The last time, the fire department had been called to get him back up, and a TV news crew had tagged along to cover the story.

Because he could no longer dress himself, he wore caftans, which were easy to slip on and off. They were immense garments, handmade, beautifully embroidered, donated by a television sitcom star with a weight problem who had heard about him on the news. (I want, the sitcom star had said, to express my solidarity with him—with big people everywhere—by contributing to his comfort in this small way.) In addition, a big-and-tall men's store had paid several tailors to make him a full suit coat, trousers, vest, a pima cotton button-down shirt, and a red and blue silk tie that was a yard and a half long. (We feel, the big-and-tall people had said, that no one—whatever their circumstances—should be deprived of a fine ensemble of clothing.) He wore this suit only once a year, when the local newspapers and TV news shows sent reporters to do their holiday stories about him, stories in which they would pity his confined existence and marvel at the tenacity of the human spirit. He didn't like doing these interviews at first. They asked the same questions every year: What is your typical breakfast? What diets have you tried? What do you do for fun? Are you happy? Are you lonely? He learned to give the answers they wanted to hear, and he played along because the publicity was good for freebies. One donor paid for his subscription to the daily paper; another took up a collection at her office to pay his utility bills; a chef at a local bistro brought him fabulous meals every year for Thanksgiving and Christmas, which prompted a chef at another restaurant to prepare an annual birthday buffet. So the interviews he got used to. But he hated wearing the suit, which the TV people insisted on. It took four volunteers two sweaty hours to get it on him, then another hour afterward to strip it off without damaging it. Mostly he wore his caftans. Once a month, a Filipina on the second floor took them to the laundromat. She and her two daughters would need most of a day to transport and launder these vast garments.

It was late afternoon and he was watching TV. He was flipping distractedly through the channels with the remote. He got free cable. (We believe, the cable people had said, that no American should be deprived of TV-viewing options.) He lived alone. He was forty-two years old. He had been honorably discharged two decades ago, returning from Southeast Asia with a medal of valor, an addiction to alcohol, and an inability to answer the question: *What now?* When he'd stopped drinking, he could not stop eating. He had found a kind of answer within his insatiable appetite. At the age of twenty-five he weighed 380 pounds, and he reached the 500 mark—joining the quarter-ton club— by his thirtieth birthday. He currently weighed just over 600 pounds. And he was at this moment very, very hungry.

He looked at the clock in the kitchenette. That bastard had left with his money over two hours ago. He had asked a neighbor, a fellow vet who lived two doors down, to go to the market for him, to buy as many packages of hot dogs—cheap, filling, and quick to eat raw—as he could with a ten-dollar bill. He knew he should not have trusted this man, a chronic boozer who'd lost his legs just below the knee and who, several times a year, would lose his prostheses as well, and could on these occasions be heard returning predawn from an all-night bender—filthy and bruised and penniless—scuttling and grunting in the stairwell, violently refusing any assistance as he made his lone and legless way five flights up.

The apartment window was open, and the curtains eddied with the onset of a breeze. He pulled up his caftan to expose himself to it, wadding yards of cloth and gathering the rolled wad onto his forearms to pinion it against his neck and shoulders. This took some work, and he was breathing hard when he was done. It was a hot one today. Days like this made him keenly aware of how badly it smelled in his apartment, much of the stink wafting from the bathroom, which the volunteers cleaned for him three times a week. Years ago, when he had finally gotten too big to leave his apartment, the members of a local church banded together and made him their special project. They deposited his monthly VA checks, shopped for his groceries, cooked him an occasional hot meal. Toward the end of the month, when he frequently ran out of food, they urged him to call. "Just give us a jingle," they chided, amused at his reluctance to summon them. They were reliable and earnest and devoutly generous, completely committed to their good works, and he could not stand having them around. They said "Howdy!" upon arrival and punctuated everything they said thereafter with either "Okey-dokey!" or "Alrighty!" When they gave him his sponge bath, or when they applied the ointments and powders prescribed for his lesions and fungal infections, they undertook these tasks with the glee of schoolchildren working a charity car wash. And they proselytized incessantly, paraphrasing biblical passages that warned against gluttony and submitting too readily to the appetites; they spoke of hunger and desire as one would speak of disreputable kin. They had given him a Bible, and reading through it—reading the whole damn book—he had found only a handful of references that warned against eating too much, but hundreds that celebrated eating and appetite. God rewarded his children with bountiful harvests, and the tribes of Israel, when not slaughtering each other, were always breaking bread. Jesus was the metaphysical short-order cook, serving up fishes and loaves and wine to multitudes wherever they gathered. And what about the Last Supper? Nobody was counting calories in the Bible. Everybody had their fill. But he did not engage this issue with them. He did not want to antagonize the people he hated needing to cook his meals and wipe his ass and offer the only companionship he had. So when he ran out of food, he did not want to give them a jingle. He tried to manage on his own, asking various transient tenants in the building to buy things for him.

He was surrounded by empty tortilla-chip bags, the partial remains of yesterday's dinner—the last time he ate. Hunger cut into his guts like a razor. He sat with his head thrown back, panting through his open mouth, waiting for another breeze. His thoughts drifted to a memory of the last time he used a bathtub as a bathtub instead of as a toilet. He thought about the last shower he ever took, and the needle-spray of water on his skin. He thought about other things he missed. Driving, with the window down. Sex. Friends. His feet. His dick. He thought about the last beach he ever saw—the smell of the ocean, its tug and surge around his calves, and the suck of wet sand under his heels. He loved the beach. He thought about his dick again. He had neither seen nor been able to touch his penis in over ten years, and he missed that.

A breeze came. He heaved the caftan roll aloft, against his face. It was a good breeze, a sudden gusty one that sent empty chip bags fluttering and was cool against his damp skin. His skin was always damp. He never stopped sweating. He lifted one tit, then the other, then let the caftan drop about him. He halfheartedly reached for an empty tortilla-chip bag, sighed, and looked from the TV screen to the clock in the kitchenette, then back to the TV. The inside of his head beat like a heart. He would have to call the church people.

He turned to look out the window. From where he sat, he could see the tops of the trees of a downtown plaza that he used to walk to and sit in, years ago. He could see the skeleton of a skyscraper that was going up. He could see the sun reflecting from an apartment tower in the distance, its light flaring in the westerly windows, then winking out as the sun moved on.

He threw the remote at the TV. A blizzard of white erupted on the screen. He reached frantically for empty tortilla-chip bags. He ripped two bags flat, licked them clean, and tossed them aside. He rocked to get at more bags. The room groaned and creaked. The love seat lurched to the left and slipped off its four-by-sixes, and he fell. Pots and plates in the kitchenette clattered. The windows shuddered in their casements when he hit the floor. He was stranded on his back. Another bag was within reach. He tore it open and licked off the oil and salt. He tossed it aside, made fists of his hands, and hit himself in the face five times.

There was activity in the apartment below, movement in the corridor outside, pounding on the door. He lay still. He did not answer. The footsteps retreated. They would be calling 911.

He sighed, wiped the blood from his face. He looked up at the window. From the floor he could see no buildings at all, only a rectangle of sky. It was cloudless and intensely blue, and he stared up into it for a long while. Emergency personnel were soon crawling over him, cutting his caftan off, lifting and pushing at his naked body, rocking it into position over their slings. It is always the same engine company that comes to his rescue, the firefighters all chatty and familiar. "How you doing, Hector?" He ignores them. He keeps his rectangle of sky in view. He sees a man on a beach ambling barefoot along the surf's edge. When the TV people arrive, with their spotlights and their boom mikes, the man on the beach breaks into a trot, angling up toward hard-packed sand. And then he turns, jogs backward for a moment, and waves goodbye—an insolent waggle of his fingers—to the people lurching through the surf behind him. He turns again without breaking stride, and he runs. He laughs. The firemen lift on three. A reporter asks why he's laughing. He doesn't hear the question. There is only the wind whistling in his ears and the sting of grit on his face and the ocean's salt taste inside his mouth. He runs, fleet and swift, the balls of his feet barely disturbing the sand and leaving no trail for anyone to follow.

They were on a blind date, arranged by a friend she worked with whose husband knew him. They had been chatting in the wine bar, waiting for a table at a popular Italian café that did not take reservations. They had been waiting over an hour, but neither of them seemed to mind, and their patience was rewarded with an intimate table, tucked into an alcove whose windows looked out on a lovely lantern-lit garden. There were long waits between menus and ordering, between salads and entrées, but they both seemed to relish the leisurely pace, which allowed the conversation to carom pleasantly from subject to subject. This was her favorite part of a date, its first few hours, when the pretense of best behavior held sway and the blemishes of individual personality had yet to appear. So things were going well. But after they ordered dessert, the subject of movies came up.

She told him about an old western she had just seen. The previous week she had been laid up with a stomach flu, unable to move or eat for days, and she watched TV the whole time. The hero was a cavalry officer, and throughout the movie he had been shooting Indians out of their saddles without batting an eye. But when he had to kill his lame horse, the hero—one of those archetypal western stoics—became hesitant and dewy-eyed.

"His name was Ol' Blue," she said. "Or Ol' Buck. The horse, I mean. And damn if I didn't start crying. It's nothing to watch people in a movie die, but when the horse gets it, I'm all weepy. Isn't that awful?"

"Not so awful," her date said. "The Indians were the bad guys. You were supposed to not care. That's how they made movies back then."

She nodded. "It still bothers me, though. People can die by the dozen, but it only gets to me when a horse or a dog is caught in the cross fire. You know what I mean?"

"I do." He leaned toward her. "I *do* know what you mean. But you see, dogs are innocent. People deserve to get it. The bad ones, anyway."

"I know," she said. The flame of a candle flickered on the table between them. She watched the light play on his face. "Sometimes I worry that I'm hardened to it. Watching human beings die while munching on popcorn."

"I don't think that would be possible with you," he said. "To be hardened, I mean."

She twirled her wineglass, looked into it, and smiled. A comfy silence arose. Dinnerware clattered quietly around them. A siren in the distance rose and fell, rose and fell.

"But then," he said, "that would depend on the human being, wouldn't it?"

She asked him what he meant. Before answering, he reached for the wine bottle, topped off her glass, and refilled his own. He leaned back in his chair.

"Let's say you're in a room," he said. "In one corner there's a dog, and in the other corner a man. A man who has killed without remorse." He sipped from his glass. She waited, her mouth slightly open.

"You have a gun," he said. "Which one do you kill? The dog? Or the man?"

She thought a moment. "That would depend on the dog," she said. "If it was one of those yippy little lapdogs? I'd plug the pooch!" She laughed.

Her blind date smiled. He carefully set his wineglass on the table. "Seriously, though. Which one would you shoot?"

She sipped from her glass, held it close. "Well, then. I wouldn't shoot either one. I would . . . abstain. That's it! I would abstain."

"But you *have* to shoot one." He leaned forward. "That's the scenario. You have the gun. One of them has to die."

"I see," she said. *Here we go*, she thought. *The fork in the road. The diverging path.* She looked out the alcove window. Moths pitched madly at the lanterns outside.

"In that case," she said, "if we have an animal and a human being, I would have to shoot the animal. That's the only choice, really." She turned to him. "Isn't it?"

He was still smiling, but blinking rapidly. "This man is a killer. He'll kill again. He has *vowed* to kill again." He leveled a finger at her. "You have to stop him from killing again."

She shook her head. "I know, but I can't point a gun at a human being and shoot him. I just can't do it." She brightened. "Say, we're both in this scenario, aren't we? Why don't I hand the gun to you?" She batted her eyes. "You'd kill him for me, wouldn't you?"

His smile widened for one second and settled into a thin line.

"All right," he said, shifting in his chair. "What's your favorite breed of dog?"

She hesitated. She had no favorite breed. She didn't like dogs, and she was about to tell him this when he snapped his fingers.

"Favorite breed," he said. "Come on, come on."

She selected a breed at random.

"Okay," he said. "Okay." He cleared a spot on the table. Near the wine bottle, a yellow Lab pup mewled adorably, gnawing on a bedroom slipper. Slouched against the candlestick, a man watched indifferently. He was, of course, a child killer, slack-jawed and cruel, with cracked lips and stains on his pants and evil in his black, greasy heart. He was the Last Child Killer. Shoot him, and all children would be safe, but let him live and he would somehow breed and multiply. Shoot the dog, and beloved Labs everywhere would vanish, never to return. Her blind date elaborated on the dire hypothetical consequences, his hands slicing the air and disturbing the candle flame. A fat moth thudded against the window glass next to his head. She watched the moth, the guttering flame, the sheen of flop sweat on her blind date's forehead.

And then dessert arrived.

It was the house specialty. They called it Cuore Inverno—a ball of hazelnut gelato inside a dark chocolate shell, drizzled with syrup of pomegranate and positioned within an immense cut-glass goblet dolloped with crème fraîche and dotted with champagne grapes. This was why she had suggested meeting at this café. She picked up her spoon and leaned forward. The man across from her had fallen silent. "Of course, it's just a game," he was saying now. "No biggie."

"Right," she said, gazing into the goblet before her. She gave the ball a sharp whack with the flat of her spoon. Ice cream oozed sweetly from the wound, and she pried into it.

"It's just interesting," he was saying. "What people would do, I mean."

She put the spoon into her mouth, sucked on it, and swallowed. She closed her eyes and groaned: "Oh. My. God." They had figured out a way to keep the gelato cold and soft while encasing it in hard chocolate. She'd been hungry all week, coming off the stomach flu. She had starved herself all day, looking forward to this evening, and it was worth it.

The man across from her touched his spoon on the table, then left it alone. "Well," he said. He looked around the café, then back at her. "This was nice," he said. "Wasn't it?" She didn't answer. He watched his blind date work intently on the dessert, watched her finish it, chattering all the while about their dinner together, speaking of it in the past tense, as if this evening had already entered their common memory, as if it had become the story they would tell their friends—the story that he imagined they would both look back upon and laugh about, years from now.

IV.

She was buried on a sun-dappled slope of lawn at the edge of the cemetery grounds, near a thin stand of cypress trees. There

were five men present: her husband, her grown son, the mortician from the funeral home, the limousine driver, and a Catholic
priest recommended by the cemetery people. They all wore
dark suits and ties, even the priest, for some reason. And they all
had on sunglasses that glinted in the midafternoon sun. They
could have been mistaken for Secret Service agents discreetly
burying one of their own. The cemetery bordered a county golf
course, and a boisterous round could be heard in progress just
over a tall hedge. When the priest closed his book and blessed
the deceased's eternal soul, the limousine driver stepped forward
and flipped a switch that engaged a pulley. As the casket de-
scended into the ground, father and son made their silent fare-
wells, and hereafter would recall this moment of departure and
loss with such ambient details as the smell of mown grass, the
twitter of a bird or two, the irregular screak of a pulley motor,
and the hoots and high fives of golfers in triumph.

In the backseat of the limousine, father and son loosened
their ties. They gazed out the windows, watching the cemetery
grounds roll away and the terrain of strip malls and auto dealer-
ships along the highway unreel past them. As their neighborhood
glided into view, the father turned away from the window, pressed
his fist between his knees, and let out a small sigh. It was a tiny,
restrained exhalation, a brief leak of air that nonetheless seemed
to deflate him completely and leave him shrunken inside his
suit. The mortician, watching in the side-view mirror, casually
wiped the corner of his eye. And even the veteran limousine
driver—a mortuary science student in his third summer with
the funeral home—even he got weepy and had to stop chewing
his gum to blink back a tear.

They pulled up in front of a small yellow house with a
gabled roof and a single dormer window that faced the street.
The stucco was chipped and patched, but the shrubs and lawn
were neatly trimmed. The mortician opened the passenger door,
and as the father and son climbed out, he asked them to wait a
moment. He went around to the trunk and hefted out a roundish,
foil-wrapped package in an open cardboard box. The mortician

was a beefy, red-faced man. He looked more like a plumber than a mortician. He stood cradling the box like an infant. Seeing as it was Thanksgiving tomorrow, he was saying, he hoped they would find use for a complimentary fifteen-pound cooked turkey, with his condolences and all the trimmings. He handed them the box, solemnly squeezed their shoulders, then climbed back into the limousine. The two of them watched the vehicle pull away from the curb, ease down the street, turn left without signaling, and disappear from view.

The father followed his son into the house, then into the kitchen. "Are you hungry, Pop?" the young man asked. He slid the heavy box onto the table in the breakfast nook and examined its contents.

"I could eat, I guess."

In addition to the turkey, there were two cans of cranberry sauce, two cans of candied yams, a quart of mashed potatoes, a loaf of soft white bread, and a pint of gravy. The son peeled back several layers of foil from the turkey to reveal a patch of crisp browned flesh, which he probed with his finger. It was still warm.

"Smells good, huh?" he said. He moved the box to the kitchen counter, lifted the turkey out, and put it back on the table. His father pulled plates and silverware out of cupboards and drawers. The boy took off his coat and rolled up his sleeves. He unwrapped the turkey until it sat brown and glistening on a bed of shredded foil. He gingerly grasped a drumstick and tugged. The turkey had been steaming in its wrapping for some time, so the leg came off easily. He set this on his father's plate and pulled the other drumstick off for himself.

The older man had since removed his coat and now sat opposite his son. "I'm really not that hungry," he said. But he began to eat anyway. He used his knife and fork to slice off small pieces, which he chewed thoroughly. His son meanwhile was holding the drumstick with both hands, biting off hunks of meat that hung out of his mouth. While the younger man appeared to be eating faster, it was the father who finished first. He ate at an unceasing pace, methodically cutting and chewing and swallowing until only a naked bone remained on his plate. He sighed and pushed it away. He patted his belly thoughtfully as he watched his son gnawing on his own drumstick. Then he got up and peered into the box on the counter.

"Do you want any of this other stuff?"

His son looked at him and grunted. So he took an opener to the cranberry sauce and candied yams, opened the mashed potatoes and gravy, and dumped their contents into separate plastic containers, microwaving each until they bubbled and steamed. The boy had gotten up and pulled two sodas from the refrigerator. He had difficulty popping the tabs with his greasy hands, and he grappled with these as his father brought all the trimmings to the table. They both began working on the turkey now. They peeled off strips of meat with their fingers and dipped them into the gravy. They spooned sauce and yams and mashed potatoes. They sopped up turkey grease from their plates with hunks of bread. They discovered a mother lode of stuffing within the turkey's cavity. "Jackpot!" the boy cried. They both lit into it, excavating with serving spoons, then abandoning decorum and reaching into the bird with their hands to pull out the stuffing in gray-brown glutinous masses. They finished two more sodas apiece, then started in on the milk, passing the half-gallon container back and forth. They stripped the bird of its meat, broke its carcass apart, and gnawed and sucked at its bones until only splinters remained scattered on the table and floor.

The window at the breakfast nook was misted from the heat of their activity. Their white dress shirts were spattered with cranberry sauce and gravy. The cuffs of their rolled-up sleeves were dark with grease. Their eyeglasses were flecked with bits of food. Their chins were shiny. They both sat dazed, gaping at each other. "Jesus H. Christ," the father gasped.

The boy scraped his chair toward the open refrigerator,

seated himself in front of it, and proceeded to rifle its contents. His father hobbled over and joined him. They found a foil-wrapped package in the freezer, hairy with ice. "Brownies!" they cried. They threw the slab into the microwave and ate it hot, with milk. They found leftover lasagna in a Tupperware container and ate it cold. They found a fried pork chop and ate it immediately, one bite each. They licked out a mixing bowl of leftover cake frosting. They ate the gluey remnants of an inde-terminate pie, the dregs of a congealing ham-and-bean soup, the desiccated remains of a forgotten noodle-cheese casserole. They pushed whatever they could find down their gullets until—engorged at last—they dropped to the floor and undid their belts and waistbands and rolled carefully onto their backs, breathing shallowly through their mouths like wounded ani-mals. A square of sunlight moved over them and slipped up the wall and disappeared into the kitchen ceiling. They gazed for some time into the corner where the light had gone, cradling and stroking their englobed bellies—their comfort against the gathering dark of a new and alien evening.

# I Run Every Day

'm up early. I'm usually awake before my alarm clock goes off, and the first thing I do is get down on the floor and stretch. I start with my legs, with the ankles and calves, then the upper hamstrings and quads. I work the muscles around the hips and the lower back. I work my neck and shoulders last. It's slow and tedious, but there's no way around that. I do the same bends and reaches in the same order for forty minutes every morning. This is my routine. This is how I wake up.

When I get outside, it's still dark. It can get pretty chilly, but I don't bundle up. Shorts and shoes and a tank top—that's all I need. I like the discomfort at the beginning of a run, when sometimes it's so cold you can't stop shaking, and every breath cuts into the back of your throat. Your knees and ankles crack and give, and the cramps stab hard. But then you find the rhythm of the run, or more accurately, you feel *it* find *you*, slipping into you like it was waiting for you along your route, and its heat spreads through you like a flame flaring up, and then the endorphins kick in and the pain is gone and everything is steady and true. There's no traffic at this hour. I run through the blinking yellow lights. I go along the boulevard under the freeway, then head into the neighborhoods above it, where the rich people live. A few of them are just getting up. I can hear their alarm clocks beep, see their lights flick on. I can see the steam rolling out of their bathroom windows. I can smell their coffee brewing. I keep going, up where the roads are unpaved and the houses are farther apart, deep in the trees. Except for the occasional yapping dog or the rumble of garbage trucks down below, it's just me up here—my breathing, the pulse in my neck, and the slap of my feet on the ground.

When I get home, the sun is out and the rest of the city is awake. I have plenty of time to cool down, stretch again, then eat and get to work by seven-thirty.

I've been at the warehouse for ten years. I started out of high school. I work on the stock floor. We're called Central Supply, and we assemble and ship orders for the county school district, everything from chalk and erasers to lightbulbs and toilet paper and basketballs on up to filing cabinets and desks. I used to be the newest guy until Ruben was hired. But they still call me the New Guy. Some kind of joke, I guess.

Ruben is about my age, and every afternoon he disappears with one of the drivers to smoke a joint out back behind the dumpsters. Ruben is Mexican, and when he first started here, he corrected us when we called him *Ru*ben, telling us that it should be pronounced Ru*ben*. From then on everybody made sure to call him *Ru*ben, which is what he goes by now.

The rest of the guys have been at the warehouse forever. Dave has been here the longest. Our foreman, Mack, says Dave came with the building—he was seventeen when he started, and it's been twenty-four years now. In a way I owe my life to

Dave. With the exception of Ruben, the men I work with are old and unhealthy. They're all overweight, and they smoke constantly, even while they eat. Dave is the worst of them. I've watched him get older and sicker—he had cancer surgery a while ago—and after a few years he started getting to me. I drank a lot then, nights after work, weekends in front of the TV. You could say I was another person back then. I lived with my folks rent-free. Nothing was expected of me. I thought I had it made. But I started worrying about things. I was afraid the warehouse would be my whole life, like it was for Dave. I counted the cigarettes he smoked and the cups of coffee he drank. I counted the sugar cubes he ate. He grabbed them by the handful and snacked on them. "Sweets for the sweet," he'd say. I watched him lick the mayonnaise off his fingers from the sandwiches his wife made him. I watched him hop down from the loading dock— a three-foot jump—and then stoop for a minute to catch his breath. I couldn't keep my eyes off him, and he got annoyed. "Am I making your heart go pitty-pat?" he said. In a way, he was. I started running that night. I went out after dark so nobody would see me. I didn't even make it around the block before I ended up puking in somebody's bushes. I thought I was going to die. My folks thought I was nuts. I kept at it, though, probably the only thing I've ever kept at.

I run every day now. I dropped forty-five pounds, and I don't drink anymore. My heart rate at rest is just under fifty beats per minute. I fall asleep every night like that, and I never need more than six hours. When I look in the mirror now, I see somebody who doesn't disgust me. I see somebody who knows the difference between what he does for a paycheck and what really matters in this life. At work Mack is always telling me to slow down. "You get paid by the hour," he says, "not by the order." I don't argue. So I slack off at work because my foreman tells me to. But I know who I am.

And I know this, too: that I owe nothing to Dave, that I owe nothing to anybody. You get where you are by yourself. There's no regret in that. That's just the way it is.

Rilke says: *Rejoice in your growth, in which you naturally can take no one with you.*


There was one person I liked. Her name was Dot, and she always referred to herself as "this old broad." She never said "I" or "me." She worked in Receiving, and I hated going in there. Receiving is full of middle-aged women, all married or widowed or divorced, and whenever I walked in, they'd stop talking and look at me with these little smiles on their faces, like I'd caught them at something. I liked Dot because when I started running, she was the first to notice the change in me, and not just losing the weight. Everybody noticed that at first. The guys said things like "You look lovely today." And even the women in Receiving made a few cracks. Dot said they didn't know anything. The body was a temple, she said, and we could all benefit from sprucing up our temples. She said I seemed calmer, settled somehow, like I'd made a decision I was comfortable with. She wasn't telling me anything I didn't know. I liked that she told it to me. She wasn't making fun of me. When she retired last summer, they had a little party for her, and she said if I ever wanted to pop a few beers with a tough old broad, to come on by. I would have. A few months later she had a stroke and had to move in with her son Phil, who works on the loading dock. Nobody has seen her since, and Phil never talks about her. If you ask him how Dot's doing, he just glares at you. So we stopped asking. If she died, I'm sure he'd tell us.

Phil's been stealing from the stock for the past year now. He hasn't been very secretive about it, and I don't know why he bothers, because it's never anything big—a few rolls of film or a box of ballpoint pens. Nobody says anything, and even Mack, who's kind of a stickler, pretty much ignores it. I guess we're all thinking the same thing: If they fired Phil, what would happen to Dot?

I suppose I was friends with Ruben once. When he first started working here and found out I ran, he told me that running was for pussies and that you had to lift weights. It was his way of inviting me to his gym. We went there one night after work, a twenty-four-hour place with a juice bar and music piped in through speakers and mirrors everywhere. Ruben introduced me around. He called me a buddy from work who was a pussy runner, and everybody laughed. I didn't get mad. I recognized this as a kind of respect. Ruben joined a group of guys around a weight machine. I never liked lifting weights. Half the time you're standing around with your hands on your hips, waiting for somebody else to finish. And then there's the mirrors, mirrors everywhere so you could watch yourself, so that everywhere you turned, there you were. One room even had mirrors on the ceiling. I got out of there and worked on a treadmill until Ruben was done. After we got cleaned up, we went out to the parking lot and joined his buddies. They were all drinking beers out of a cooler in somebody's car trunk. They were talking about the women in the gym, about who was hot and all that. And I guess in all the talk I let a few things slip. It wasn't the beer. I only had one bottle. So it wasn't the beer. It's just that when you're talking and everybody's having a good time, when people are talking to you and everything feels okay, you just let your guard down. I should have known what to expect from people. I should have known better.

Later that week, Eugene sat down next to me at lunch and handed me a doughnut and asked if I wanted a moment alone with it. I didn't get it. Then Ruben slid the whole box over, a big pink box filled with doughnuts and little packs of condoms. They called it the virgin assortment, and they said I had to fuck every doughnut before attempting real pussy. Then Dave put his cigarette down and stood up. They'd cut one of his lungs out, and he was still smoking. He stood up and pumped at the table with his hips, and said the best woman he ever had anyway was a butterscotch custard bar. Mack finally told them to knock it off, and they did, and he changed the subject. But nobody was listening to him. They were all sitting there, grinning down into their thermoses and ashtrays. They were having a great time.

That was it for me. I eat by myself now, out on the loading dock. Mack didn't like that at first. He said it creates discord. "You have to eat chow with your shipmates," he told me. But since I still take breaks with them, he lets me eat lunch alone. I've got a spot at the far end of the dock where they recharge the fork-lifts and pallet movers at night. I can catch the last of the noon-time sun before it swings to the other side of the building. I like it out here in the fresh air, in the sunlight, away from the smoke and the smell from the crap they heat up in the microwave.

I've lived in this house my whole life. My folks died here. They both got cancer, my mother first and then my father, and I took care of them both and now they're gone. So the house is mine. I have a brother who wants nothing to do with it. He's a law-yer for the EPA up in Alaska. We were never close. Lately he's been calling me once a month or so, out of the blue, to say hello. He doesn't have to. I tell him that, but he still calls. He says he wants to come down for a visit sometime, to bring his family. He says he wants his kids to meet their uncle. I tell him: "Fine, come down whenever."

I've taken good care of this house. Whatever it's needed, I've done. I sanded and planed and lacquered the floors a few years ago, and I did a pretty good job. I keep the lawn and the bushes trimmed and neat, and the neighbors appreciate that. They tell me so. These are things I care about. I don't own a TV; I don't watch that crap. I listen to the radio and I read the news-papers every day, so I know what's going on in the world. And I don't need anybody telling me how a life is supposed to be. I'm alone, but I'm not lonely; there's loneliness and then there's solitude, which is a positive thing. *It is good to be solitary, for solitude is difficult.* Rilke said that. I've read him. I read books. I know who I am.


The new girl's name was April. She was hired to replace Dot, and on her first day Mack brought her out to meet us. The guys were very polite. They told her about the rooftop bowling alley and tried to sell her tickets to the underground swimming pool. It was the same routine they did on my first day, and when Ruben was hired. But when she and Mack left, they started in on how fat she was. Phil said you'd have to roll her in flour first to fuck her, just to find the wet spot.

She started coming out onto the stock floor regularly, to chat and to hang out during breaks. This was a new thing for us. The women in Receiving rarely came out onto the floor, and then only to ask where Mack was and then go looking for him. None of them ever came out otherwise. There was no policy against it. It just didn't happen. The guys muttered to each other when they saw April heading our way. "Here comes our mascot," they said. "Here comes the pooch." They were nice to her when she came around. They told their jokes and their stories, and she laughed and told a few of her own, and they laughed. But when she was gone, they leered and made fun of her. They were always talking about screwing her, but not in a good way. And they wouldn't let up on the fat jokes. I didn't get it, because she wasn't that fat, no fatter than any of them. I thought at first that if she dropped a few pounds, maybe they would've let up on her. Maybe things would've been different. But they just find something else about you to make fun of. It's what they do. They're good at it.

April went out for lunch. She always went alone. If she got back early, she'd spend the rest of her hour with the guys on the stock floor. She didn't socialize much with the women in Receiving. She was the youngest one in there.

A few weeks after she started, she came up on the dock on her way back from lunch. "So," she said to me, "you're the New Guy." She lit a cigarette and asked me why I ate alone. I told her it was because of the cigarette smoke inside. She looked at the cigarette she'd just lit, and laughed. And she put it out. From then on, just about every day, she swung by and talked to me, fiddling with an unlit cigarette. I had nothing to say, but she didn't seem to mind. She was a talker. She told me that. "So that makes you the listener," she said. So she talked, and I listened, sitting on the dock while she stood leaning against a stack of pallets. When I got tired of squinting up at her, I looked at my food. Sometimes I looked out over the lot, where you could see the heat wiggle up from the blacktop. It was hot that summer. April had just moved here, and I remember her saying how she was discovering the place, getting to know the bus system, finding the neighborhood pubs and the secondhand shops, doing all the tourist things. She rode the dinner train up to the capital once and did the tour of the abandoned prison over in Old Town. She went to the zoo. I hadn't been there since I was a kid. They charged admission now. And they were getting rid of the cages. There was an Otter Island, and a Gorilla Haven. The cats where getting their own places, too, a savanna for the lions and grottoes with pools for the panthers and tigers. I was born here, and April already knew more about the city than I ever would.

Sure enough, the guys started in on me. Eugene wanted to know if she was a moaner or a screamer. Dave asked if we had set a wedding date, and if we were registered at any of the doughnut shops. Ruben laughed with the rest of them. But whenever we were alone, he said I should ask April out. He said that she wanted me and that it would be a waste to not go for it. I told him I didn't even like her. "Fuck like," he said. "What's like got to do with anything?" He wouldn't leave it alone. He wouldn't leave *me* alone. I'd be working the floor and he'd be running up and down the aisles looking for me, whispering at me through the shelving that pussy was a gift from God, or cornering me with his cart to tell me that I had a duty as a man. We hadn't said ten words to each other in years, and here he was getting all worked up about my duty as a man. I never liked Ruben. Who was he to tell me about being a man? Who was he to tell me anything?

She asked me about my running. I told her. I kept it simple, sticking to my regimen, telling her what I do and not getting near why I do it. She was playing with her unlit cigarette while I talked, flipping and catching it in her hand. But she was listening. So I told her she could do it, too, if she wanted. She was about my age, maybe younger, so it wouldn't take long to get a routine going, and to see results. She just smiled and shook her head. She put the cigarette she was playing with in her mouth and lit it. "I lack discipline," she said. "Which is something you've got a lot of." She blew a thin stream of smoke above her head and swatted at it to keep it away from me. She was right. It *was* something I had a lot of.

Another time she brought it up again. She asked about my regimen, and it turned into this interrogation. She wanted to know what time I got up every morning and how long I stretched for. She wanted to know how long I spent on my calves, on my thighs, on my neck. She asked what direction I headed in when I ran and what streets I turned on and whether I took the same streets back. She stood above me with the sun at her back and fired her questions at me. I answered every one of them. It was kind of a game, like a lawyer and a witness, and I let myself get caught up in it because I thought she really wanted to know about what I did, that the details of my regimen, and my absolute knowledge of them, were bringing her around somehow. I was wrong. She bent down all of a sudden, real quick, and leaned in close. I could smell her hair. I could've looked down her blouse if I wanted to. And she said, "Well, maybe discipline

is something a person can have too much of. Don't you think?"
And the way she was looking at me, I realized she wasn't inter-
ested in running at all. I didn't say anything. She straightened
up and checked her watch and walked back inside. Lunch was
over.

She was looking at me like she knew something about me,
as if you could know a person just by looking in his face. She
thinks she knows me. She doesn't know anything about me.
I've looked at my face. You can't see anything in it.


Here's something about me. I was running around the lake one
afternoon when this woman fell into step alongside me. She ran
well, with her legs in full extension. She clipped along in smooth,
even strides, her shoulders slack and her arms relaxed, swing-
ing in little arcs along her rib cage. There wasn't a single wasted
motion about her. She ran with me. We didn't say a word. After
four laps around she tapped me on the shoulder. She smiled and
said thanks. I watched her pull off and head down a path toward
the streets. I went to the lake regularly for a few months after
that. I never saw her again.

When you run, you aspire to an economy of motion that
has only one goal: to optimize the intake of oxygen so that you
can keep running. Anything that impedes this one goal must
fall away.

I don't remember the woman's face anymore. All I remember is the way she moved, the way everything about her was
contained and effortless and perfect. Sometimes I imagine her
alongside me when I run, and I try to match my every movement
to hers. Our shoulders jostled each other when we rounded the
turns that day. Her hair was in a single braid, a thick rope of hair
that swayed across her back. You could hear it swish against her
windbreaker. The rhythm of it paced us both.

When I told Dot about this woman, I remember her sighing
and shaking her head, telling me to just let it go. If more people

did that, she said, if they just left each other alone, there'd be less disappointment in this world. I've realized that everything Dot ever told me, all of her advice for me, came from somebody I didn't know much about. I knew her husband was dead and that she had other kids besides Phil. They came up in passing when we talked. She never said anything bad about them, but she never said anything good about them, either. I didn't know if she had any grandkids. I didn't know what she did outside of work. I didn't even know where she lived. Dot never smiled. "Bad teeth," she told me once. But I remember her smiling when she told me this—the only time I'd seen her do that—and her teeth were fine. She didn't sleep well, so she was always tired, and she moved around the office carefully, hanging on to the edges of desks and cabinets. She was a small woman, but she moved with this weight in her, like her gravity was different from everybody else's, as if it took everything she had just to get across the room or to get through the day.

When I told Dot about the woman at the lake, she said as long as I was happy, why chance it with anybody else? Why risk what you've got for something you may never have?


So we went on a date. April caught me after work and asked if I wanted to buy her a drink. She gave me directions to a place she knew. "Turn right here," she said. "Left up there." She used her unlit cigarette as a pointer. She said she liked my car. It's a '69 Olds that belonged to my father, and he took good care of it. Change the oil every three months, he'd told me, wash it every other week, catch all the rust spots before they spread—do that and a car will last forever. That's what my father taught me. April said that's a good tradition to have, keeping the family car in shape.

The bar we went to was on a frontage road that looped north of the airport. It reminded me of every other bar I'd ever been in, with carved-up tables and wobbly chairs and ratty love seats against the wall. There were TVs mounted in the ceiling corners, all of them on, and a jukebox going, and people hooting around the pool tables in the back. And there was the smell of the place. I read somewhere that smell is the most primitive of the senses, that it can trigger memory more strongly and deeply than any other sense. This bar had that smell, and it all came back to me. Just because you change your life doesn't mean you don't miss things.

We sat at the bar, and the guy behind it knew April by name and gave her the usual, a vodka gimlet. I had orange juice. I wanted a beer. I admit that. But I didn't have any beer that night. Beer had nothing to do with it.

She handed her cigarettes to me and told me to ration her. "I'm cutting down," she said. And then she just started telling me things—where she was born, where her folks were born, what they did for a living. She had three sisters and two brothers, and she told me what they all did for a living. Some of what she said I never would have guessed. She was married once. She called her ex-husband The Mistake. And she had a kid somewhere, who she never saw because The Mistake was such a dick. But she thought about the kid all the time. She was learning how to crotchet, taking a class in it at the extension college. And she was a big reader, mysteries and true crime. "You know, crap," she said. Then she ordered us another round and said, "Okay, your turn." So I told her where I was born, where I went to high school. I told her about my folks being dead and what I've done to the house, fixing it up. I didn't have much else to say after that. But again, she didn't seem to mind. She asked me a few questions—what did I do in high school, what did I do for fun. When I couldn't answer, she just asked me for a cigarette instead, and held it out for me to light, and thanked me.

The bar was getting busy. Everybody was coming up and saying hello to her. Her life seemed filled with people, crowded with them. Somebody shouted her name from the back, where the pool tables were. "Come on," she said, "let's play." I told her to go ahead. "Come *on*," she said again. "One game." She put her hand on top of mine and said she'd teach me. But I told her to go play pool, and I guess she got the way I said it, because she held her hands up. "Okay, Okay," she said.

There was a baseball game on the TV. Two guys next to me were watching it, and whenever anything happened, they hollered and banged their fists on the bar. One of them kept elbowing me accidentally and apologizing for it. Sure enough, he knocked my orange juice over. He apologized again and bought a round. He sent April's drink to her. He told me that April was a great gal. I looked over at where she was, and when she got her drink, she bowed to us, and me and the guy next to me waved back. I watched her back there. She was having a good time, getting drunk. They all were. I turned back to the TV.

After a while I felt something on my leg, and when I looked down, I saw April's hand, sitting there on my knee. She leaned on it and slid into her barstool. "I won," she said. She leaned into me and laughed. Her hair was against my face. She was asking how we were doing, how things were going with us. I told her: "Fine, things are fine." She was saying that she liked me, that she liked the shy ones. She was telling me this with her mouth next to my ear. I could feel her breath. I looked over at the drink she had put down on the bar. The glass was smeared with her lipstick all around the rim and halfway down the side.

So I told her about the guys making fun of her behind her back. She stiffened up, then pulled away to look at me. It was like she'd sobered up immediately, as if I'd just come into focus in front of her. "Tell me something I don't know," she said. I didn't expect that—that she knew. I asked her how she could let them degrade her like that, how she could think so little of herself. "Why do you put up with it?" I asked her. And she smiled her little smile and said, "Same reason you do." Then she grabbed her cigarettes and her drink and went back to play pool with her friends.

We didn't talk anymore after that. I sat at the bar and waited for her to finish her game so we could get out of there. I watched TV. The baseball game was over. I don't remember what was on after that. But I remember watching something, and drinking my orange juice, and eating the ice.

It was raining outside. The streetlights had just come on, and you could see the drizzle swirling down around them. The weather was strange that summer. There'd been a funnel cloud a few weeks before. I remember reading about it bouncing around the downtown area, blowing out windows and tipping over newspaper racks, trying to touch ground, they said, trying to become a tornado.

April was drunk, and walking wobbly. My car was a block or so up the street, and by this time it was the only one there. A chain-link fence separated it from an airfield. All the cargo companies were up here, and some of their planes were out, roaring around the tarmac, their lights flashing through the mist.

When we got in the car, I asked her where she lived. She looked at me from her side of the front seat, all woozy, but giving me that look she gave me that day on the dock. She slid over toward me, and it seemed to take a while. The seats in an Olds are bench seats, and long, like sofas. And when she finally got to me, she said my name and kissed me on the mouth. I admit that I let her. I let her because I've never heard my name said the way she was saying it, and because it's been a long time since anybody's touched me. Her mouth just slipped onto mine, and it was nothing like I'd imagined, and I let myself get all caught up in it, in this feeling that you're part of a world with other people in it, and that you matter because somebody else seems to think you do. Her mouth was soft and warm. But it reeked of cigarettes and fruity lipstick, and when I opened my eyes, there she was—April from work, with her face up against mine, telling me how we were two of a kind and how we needed to do something about that, her and me. She put her hand on my neck. I felt it hover there, small and light. I smacked it away and I gave her a shove. She ended up on her side of the seat, holding her hand like I'd hurt it. Who was she to say we were alike? There's *nothing* of her in me. So I did something about it, about her and me. I pushed the seat back and got her down on it. She may have been yelling, but I'm not sure anymore, because it got really loud with the rain coming down hard and the planes outside roaring around like they were coming right on top of us. I kept one hand on her mouth and I started working down there with the other one until she stopped struggling, and she just lay there and let me finish. When I was done, she eased out from under me and slid back to her side of the seat. She sat there for a minute with her head against the passenger window, like she was listening for something in the rain outside. It was really coming down now. And when she started putting herself back together, I told her to tell me where she lived.

She sat smoking her cigarettes the whole way. When we got to her apartment building, I waited until she got inside okay. Then I cracked all the windows to air out the car for the drive home. Then I drove home.

She was late the next morning. She came in with her wrist taped up. She told the guys she sprained it falling out of bed. They loved that. She's still friendly with them, but doesn't talk to me anymore. For a while Dave was coming up, putting his arm around me, and asking if the honeymoon was over, if the bloom was off the rose.

She doesn't talk to me anymore. But she doesn't avoid me, either. At lunchtime she still comes in and out through the back lot and up the dock. I'm at my usual spot, and she'll go up the steps, then stop and light a cigarette before going inside. She looks right at me the whole time.

So I eat my lunch in my car. It's at the far end of the lot, back where the busted pallets are piled. From where I'm parked I can see her come in. I can see her walk past where I used to sit. My not being there doesn't faze her at all. She just gets on with her life. When she's gone, I get out and grab a few minutes on the dock before going back to work, a few minutes of sun at least, before it moves over the building, and then only until the fall. By early winter the sun's too low and doesn't hit the dock at all.

I've started a new routine. On the weekends I go up into the mountains for a long run. I've got water bottles stashed in hiding places up there. I drive up and replenish them once a month. Above the tree line the roads end in cul-de-sacs, and from then on it's nothing but fire trails that switchback through scrub and grass and rock. I take it easy getting up there, but once I hit the trailheads, I pour it on. I pound up that grade and I don't ease up until I reach the plateau.

I go all day in those mountains. I've gotten lost up there. Sometimes I don't get back until after nightfall, so depleted, so close to the brink, that it takes everything I've got to just hang on and make it home. I'm weaving and staggering along, and I'm laughing. People have pulled over and gotten out of their cars to ask if I'm okay. They think there's something wrong because sometimes I can't stop laughing. But there's nothing wrong. Sometimes that's just how good I feel.

# Somoza's Dream

He is scuttling through the dark. His bare foot steps into something cold and slick. His leg shoots forward. He skids. The ground beneath him is suddenly gone. Synapses fire, nerve bundles twitch, and he is falling. Muscles spasm in myoclonic response. His legs jitter under the sheets. Dinorah, lying next to him, crabs away. Then an alarm, sharp and jangly. He stirs, and his tumble ceases. He reaches for the clock, kills it. Through eye slits, a vast room takes shape in the chocolate dark. Drapes as thick as hides cover ceiling-high windows. Morning light bleeds in. He snorts, hawks, swallows. He awakes, knows now where he is. His room. This world. Today: Wednesday, September 17, 1980.

The Presidente-in-Exile rises.

In the bathroom, post-shower, post-shave. He steps on the spring scale. The needle flutters shyly below one seventy-five. Not bad. He gives his belly a small-caliber-gunshot slap. "Not bad at all," he says.

In the dressing room, his fingers glide through a kelp of neckties, fondling the Zegnas, stroking a yellow jacquard. He snaps it out, runs it through his collar. He speed-dials Bettinger, puts him on speakerphone, confirms their appointment while finishing up the knot—nine sharp, Van Damm's office at the Banco Alemán. "The fix is in, Tacho," Bettinger says. He pads to the shoe closet, selects a pair of burgundy loafers, Russia calf Henleys. "The bitch is prone," Bettinger purrs. "Knees up and ready for fucking." He drops the shoes to the carpet, kicks them parallel, steps daintily into them. He slips the heels with an ivory-handled shoehorn. Bettinger is prattling on. The Presidente-in-Exile secures his cuff links. He moves to the dressing-room window, looks down into the courtyard two stories below, dingy and penumbral in pre-morning light. He can make out the white Mercedes parked under the eaves of a tree, a palsy of branches like crone's hands poised above the vehicle. His eyes adjust, and he can now see the pink turds of sticky blossoms splattered on the roof and windshield. Bettinger is detailing financial arrangements—float risks and laundry fees and yield guarantees. He smarms and panders on speakerphone like an obscene caller. The Presidente-in-Exile cuts him off and speed-dials Gallardo. He can hear the phone ringing below, in the quarters over the carriage house. He slips a titanium clip over the tie's face, secures a matching tie bar under the knot. When Gallardo picks up, he tells his driver to stop parking under that fucking tree and to get that shit cleaned off the car now.

In the bedroom, he gives his suit coat a dervish whirl and slips into it. He approaches the bed, leans down. He kisses Dinorah goodbye, reminds her about lunch. She burrows away, deep into the bedding. Body heat purls off her. She sleeps like a dead man. It is a thing about her he admires.

In the kitchen, the Presidente-in-Exile's egg is boiling. It ticks in a pot of water on the range. Cook cuts a small grapefruit in two. She Saran-wraps one half for the fridge, washes the other, and pats it dry. A timer goes *ding*. She reaches into the boiling water with her fingers, plucks out the egg, holds it under the cold tap for five seconds, then seats it in its special cup. Cook is a tiny woman, a Guaraní Indian of indeterminate age with jet-black hair, the hard palms of a tenant farmer, and skin as dark and smooth as burnished jatoba wood. She lays out breakfast on a tray—soft-boiled egg, grapefruit, two pink packets of Sweet'N Low, two tablespoons of cottage cheese on a Ry-Krisp, six ounces of orange juice. Also, the London *Financial Times*. Also, three aspirin; he was out and about late last night. An egg spoon, a grapefruit knife, a cloth napkin. Almost ready. Cook positions a single locust-wood toothpick on a tiny copper salver. She then leans over the grapefruit, purses her lips, and releases a modest pearl of spit onto its glistening surface. Breakfast is served.

On the west patio, the Presidente-in-Exile prowls through the newspaper. The sun has just broken the ridge high above the villa. It is light and already warm. *"Buen desayuno, patrón,"* Cook murmurs as she places the tray before him. He rattles his paper. He does not speak to Cook, who came with the villa. She retreats, returns to the kitchen to prepare luncheon. Guests are expected today—that Italian, Bettinger, and some others from the bank. No breakfast for the mistress. A late sleeper, Dinorah has yet to see the sun rise in Paraguay.

The Presidente-in-Exile repasts. He snaps a page of *El Diario*. There's been nothing about him lately, thank Christ. Since his arrival fourteen months ago, the Asunción dailies have cut him no slack. Every indiscretion is rooted out and blown out of proportion—shopping sprees, drunken romps, shoving matches with cops and maître d's, public squabbles with Dinorah. The trivia of his life as a private citizen is made public, laid out to be probed and pawed at. They went through his garbage once, and the guards caught them red-handed, knocked them around a bit, and *that* was reported—brutal suppression of the press or some such bullshit. Last year the service main in the street burst, leaving him without water for days. He called Stroessner in a fury to complain, to simply get it taken care of. The papers reported that he called the president of Paraguay to fix his plumbing. They hate him here. They think him arrogant and crass. They think he "sullies the dignity of the Republic." Sullies! That's what the papers have said! And Stroessner is no fan, either; otherwise he wouldn't let them write that shit. But Stroessner has extended his protection. And Stroessner has been well paid. But they do hate him here.

Well, fuck them. He hates them, too.

He works on his grapefruit, browses the paper. There is a full-page ad with the banner headline DO YOU RECOGNIZE THIS MAN? It offers a reward for information on the whereabouts of Nazi war criminal Josef Mengele. The Presidente-in-Exile snorts, flips the page. Sully my balls! Dignity of the Republic, my ass! Hideout for Nazis, haven for cocaine kings. There is an opinion piece by an undersecretary of the Ministry of the Interior railing against the feral dog population and concluding with an appreciation of the dictator Francia, who in 1840 ordered every dog in Paraguay killed. And there is an item buried in Business Briefs, a report on unanticipated delays with a hydroelectric project down on the Argentine border, involving work stoppages and a cement embargo. Bettinger's little venture— some kind of deal with the unions that will work to his financial advantage. Leave it to Bettinger: *The bitch is prone.* The Presidente-in-Exile lets *El Diario*'s pages spill to the ground. He looks at his watch. He spoons the guts of his egg onto the cottage cheese, picks up the Ry-Krisp, and pushes it all into his mouth. He licks his fingers and wipes them with the napkin. He tosses back the orange juice and smacks his lips. "Ahhh!" He stands up, tucks the *Times* under his arm; it is air-expressed from São Paolo every morning and delivered to the villa from the airport by taxicab.

He strolls across the patio, then stops short. Something flits into the edge of his vision, and he turns. He spots it, hovering, then alighting upon the ground. He approaches. It is some kind of insect, a big one. Thin, translucent wings spanning half a foot shimmer and iridesce in morning light. Perpendicular to these, a thorax over seven inches long inscribes in the air a slender and delicate arc of the deepest red—the red of arterial blood, of crème de cassis and rubies and the juice of roasted meat. It is a helicopter damselfly, the rarest of the order Odonata in all the world, and far from its range in southwest Brazil. The Presidente-in-Exile would not know this. He bends down, eyes narrowed. "What the fuck," he mutters, for he has never in his life seen anything like it. He peers intently, seemingly making a study of this rare and exquisite creature—a trembling scarlet wound against the gray slate tiles. He pivots his left foot and moves the thin leather sole of his bespoke shoe centimeters above it. He taps. There is a sound like a burst of static, and the insect is squashed like a bug. The Presidente-in-Exile proceeds across the patio, dragging his foot once to scrape off the gore. He cuts through the west garden, along a flagstone pathway that circles toward the front of the villa. Behind him, the discarded pages of his newspaper trip and tumble across the grounds in a zephyr that has come from nowhere on this still and windless day.

In the courtyard, Gallardo has moved the Mercedes out from under the tree. The Mercedes is an armored vehicle custom-equipped with hardened steel body panels, 1.5-inch-thick windows of polycarbonate ballistic glass, and Kevlar-lined gas tanks. Gallardo has just finished the washing, and the car glistens all dewy in the light. He is struggling with the water hose, trying to coil it without getting his dress shirt dirty. Ten yards away, outside the gate, on Avenida España, a red Datsun blocks the driveway to the villa. Three men loll on the car, smoking cigarettes. They call to Gallardo: *"Maricón, chuparosa, marica chingada."* They blow him kisses. They tell him they have hoses for him to handle, if he wishes. These men are the Paraguayan body-guards assigned by Stroessner to protect the Nation's Esteemed Guest. Gallardo snaps his wrist, flicks his finger, fires his cigarette butt. It traces an arc through the bars of the gate and lands in a burst of embers on the chest of the biggest guard. Direct hit. Beautiful. The guard leaps off the Datsun, curses, rushes the gate. But what can he do? Gallardo smiles, turns around, and waggles his ass. The guard reaches down and grabs his crotch. A piercing high-pitched whistle disrupts their pas de deux. From the pathway into the gardens, the Presidente-in-Exile is waving his folded paper impatiently: Let's go. The driver kicks the hose into the bushes, slips into his coat, gets in the Mercedes and starts it up. The bodyguards squeeze into the Datsun and back the car out of the way. The gates glide open. The Mercedes exits. The Datsun follows. The gates close. Overhead, security cameras mounted atop thirty-foot poles turn slowly, taking in the perimeter with a ho-hum weariness.

In the backseat, the Presidente-in-Exile excavates his ear canal with the locust-wood toothpick. Eyes closed, he grunts blissfully. Out his passenger window, a sun-strobed flip-book of Asunción—whitewashed brick walk-ups along tree-lined avenues, nannies pushing prams, *chipa* vendors pushing carts, barefoot women with towers of folded laundry on their heads, white-suited old men walking tiny old dogs, sanitation workers in yellow coveralls sweeping dirt into the gutters. And everywhere, the guano-crowned statuary of the Republic's military heroes.

By the time they reach the Plaza of the Chaco War, the *señor*'s face is buried in the *Times* and Gallardo has shaken the bodyguards. He's not supposed to do this. It pisses off the Minister of Security. But Gallardo gets bored, and it's fun, although too easy now since Stroessner's monkeys have been downgraded to that piece-of-shit Datsun. And besides, the *señor* doesn't care. Gallardo negotiates the traffic circle—an apocalyptic teem of limos and buses and taxicabs, dray trucks and trailer rigs, and the intrepid horse-drawn wagon. On Avenida Mariscal López, he slows the Mercedes for the left onto Calle America, one of the intersections in the city with a traffic signal. The lights are his, and he would have made it but for a turquoise blue Chevy pickup that backs out of a driveway and lurches to a halt in the street. Gallardo hits the brakes. He sighs, gives his horn a toot. The truck that cuts him off is shotgunned with mud, a ferrous earth of unsettling redness. Gallardo remembers his first look at Paraguay, peering out the porthole of the Learjet that brought them here, the Gran Chaco below him, the high desert pan that makes up the western half of this country. Flat and featureless and still, it burned red under the sun. As far as the eye could see, an ocean of blood in its doldrums. It was another world. *His* world now, he thought.

The truck does not move. Gallardo toots again, and at this moment—seconds before the rocket hits the Mercedes—he apprehends two nearly simultaneous events. The first, he sees: the driver of the truck—a woman, a redhead, maybe—ducking down out of sight. And the second, he hears, even with the armored-glass windows rolled up and the AC turned up full: a brief and powerful susurration in the air, like a sudden wind in the trees or the exhalation of a thousand breaths. It is the last thing the Presidente-in-Exile's driver hears.

One block west, the red Datsun accelerates out of its turn onto Mariscal López just as a fireball rises up ahead, followed by the concussion waves of the explosion. The driver of the Datsun leans on the horn, punches the gas pedal, cuts through traffic. The man next to him pounds the dashboard. The guards in the car draw their pistols, unlock and crack open the doors. They are screaming and cursing. They curse God. They curse the Minister of Security for replacing their Ford Falcons and Gran Torinos with fucking Datsuns, and curse their own mothers for bringing them into a world of bureaucrats and bean counters. And they are weeping, expelling violent and angry tears for their derailed careers, for that *puto* Gallardo smeared all over the street up ahead, and for the lost honor of the Glorious Republic of Paraguay.

In the backseat of the Mercedes, the Presidente-in-Exile looks up from his paper.

Gallardo's arms fly up over his head in a referee's goal signal of such ferocity that the arms tear off his shoulders. Gallardo's head disappears. In its place, blood-gout from the neck like a dark, wet rose. Pieces of Gallardo fly up the hole in the roof, through three layers of armored steel flayed back. And the Presidente-in-Exile follows, in a geyser of metal and meat, glass and bone. Up and away.

The Presidente-in-Exile rises.


His nickname was Tacho. In history he is referred to as Tacho II—"Tacho Dos"—to distinguish him from his father, the previous Presidente. The domestic press used to call him El Tachito, a diminutive that implied an unfavorable comparison. This was back when the press got away with such things, before reporters started disappearing. Until the mid-1970s, officials in the U.S. State Department called him the legitimate president of his country, for he was a vocal critic of Castro's Cuba and thus a friend to the American people. The expatriate opposition called him *bruto, monopolista*, America's Fart-Sniffing Lapdog. His self-bestowed title was *jefe supremo*, and everyone in his administration referred to him as such. But he allowed the *comandantes* of *la Guardia Nacional* to address him as *señor jefe*, or simply *señor*, an informality that revealed his soft spot for the glory days, when he was once a *comandante* among them. He liked to think that this gesture put them at ease. For they were his men, his *compadres*. They drank and whored with him. But they were never at ease with him. He was volatile and petulant, a man of brittle temperament. If you brought him bad news, you were doomed. He would shove members of his cabinet, slap documents out of their hands. He would throw food at banquets, snap pencils in two, sweep the contents of laden desktops to the floor. It was said he could barely speak Spanish. This was not true; he simply preferred English, calling it his mother tongue. He was schooled in America, in a military academy on Long Island, then at West Point, where he was—by mandate of the Undersecretary of State for Central American Relations—a 4.0

student. He was hazed by the upperclassmen in the name of unit loyalty and cohesion. Very often a line was crossed, and the rituals took on an erotically charged brutality. But he accepted the abuses and humiliations because he believed in the tradition of abuse and humiliation. These men did not care who he was or who his father was. He was simply a puke to them, and initiated as brutally—no more and no less—as the others were. This is what makes you a part of the whole. A puke among pukes, you become a man among men. He took little else from his formal military schooling except this, and a penchant for fancy titles and uniforms, and a love of World War II movies: *Patton*, *The Guns of Navarone*, *The Great Escape*, *The Dirty Dozen*, *Hell in the Pacific*. He was a fan of the actor Lee Marvin. He met him once at a Hollywood benefit for earthquake relief and pestered him for an autograph. The actor was drunk and belligerent, but accommodated him, and scrawled on a grimy dinner napkin:

To the President of N_____
Piss up a rope, you bastard
Lee Marvin


When his presidency was toppled and he was run out in 1979, he was the majority stockholder of the national air and rail lines. He owned the beef ranches and the meat-processing plants, the timber tracts and the lumber mills. Coffee, cotton, bananas, sugar, tobacco, rice—from field to factory to export, it all belonged to him. Near the end, President Carter had asked him to give some of it back, to return something of his plunder— *any*thing—as a concession to history: "As a personal favor to me, Tacho." He called the president of the United States a bastard and told him to piss up a rope. His wife was an American citizen living in Miami Beach. When he joined her there and the Carter administration asked him to leave, she stayed. She was the daughter of diplomats, a graduate of Barnard and Columbia, and had always hated his nickname. Tacho! She thought it lowborn and tawdry—a gangster's moniker. She alone among his intimates addressed him by his Christian name. Soon after their marriage she never addressed him by name at all. Within five years they lived in separate houses; within fifteen, separate countries. Yet they had five children together, who all called him *papi*. And although he was an absent father, they seemed genuinely fond of him. They were born and schooled in the United States; he joked once that he wanted them to amount to something, that the run of dictators in the family had to end. To hear an utterance such as this, wry and self-effacing, come out of a man like him was an extraordinary and unsettling event, a paradox—like a blossom from a cinder block—whose occurrence only affirmed its own impossibility. For the truth was this: he was a resolutely dull man. When he walked into a room, there was no effect. He looked like a barber or a haberdasher, and so it was standard procedure to announce his entrances to generate the appropriate hubbub and attention. He boasted that he was a hard-ass, a control freak, a micromanager obsessed with the details. He said he wanted to know *every*thing. But when you'd tell him, he'd get bored. At cabinet meetings and security briefings he would gaze out the window at the squirrels in the trees, or release gaping yawns without covering his mouth, or intently go through his coat pockets looking for something. Then, out of sheer impatience, he would cut the meeting short and hastily okay whatever was being discussed—diplomatic policy, military ops, orders of arrest and interrogation. Yet he could spend hours shopping for socks. He could fritter away an afternoon picking out the *perfect* wallet. He had health concerns. A heart attack at age forty-two scared the bejesus out of him. He was told to drop seventy pounds. He did, and he kept it off. But he bickered constantly with his doctors, fussing over his meds and his course of treatment. He obeyed them, of course. He was too scared not to. He had digestive problems—chronic intestinal gas and acid reflux—which he frequently mistook for an incipient heart attack. He brooded. He was always vaguely preoccupied or in a sulk about something. His children called him Sourpuss, Grumpy Gus, Señor Mopey-Pants. When he was booted from the United States, his mistress of twelve years, a former rental car agent and part-time model named Dinorah Sampson, joined him in the Bahamas. When denied sanctuary there, they were taken in by Paraguay. Dinorah had numerous names for him that ran the gamut of moods: Big Bear, Big Bull, *cabrón pinche, cabrón* Cocksucker, Lying Cocksucker Dog, My Prince, My Light, My One True Love. And swaying above him in bed, rotating gently against his decorous thrusts—for the heart attack had made him an overcautious lover—she called him *bestia. "Mi bestia amor,"* she would whisper, leaning down, the warmth of her breath in his ear and the rasp of her cheek on his in the thick hush of the villa around them. *Bestia amor, mi corazón feroz.* My beast, my beloved. My savage, my heart.


The Presidente-in-Exile is watching his mistress swim.

He reclines in a chaise by the pool. He wears slippers and white linen slacks and a cream guayabera. His legs are crossed at the ankles, slim and pale as a girl's. Inside the slippers—Bergamo-silk-lined morocco loafers—his feet are bare, powdered and smooth, the heels exfoliated, the nails squared and buffed. He sips a Walker Blue Label on the rocks and pretends to read prospectuses, a batch of them in his lap. Bettinger insists on this, Bettinger always with a hard-on for the windfall scheme, the in-and-out deal, the killing: "They all want you, Tacho." And they do. They all want his participation. Every cover letter says so: "We would be *so* pleased with your participation"; "Your participation is anxiously anticipated." He is in fact meeting to-morrow morning with people who want him, an investors group at the Banco Alemán.

The Presidente-in-Exile yawns. It is near dusk, too dark to read anything. But he pretends, thumbing through a folder while, from the corner of his eye, he watches his mistress swim. She has packed on the pounds since their arrival in Asunción. He has told her: "Where is the woman I fell in love with? Where did this *cow* come from?" Sometimes he moos at her. It embarrasses him to watch her cross a room, galumphing and tottering to find her center of gravity in stiletto heels. But in the water she is supple and dolphin-sleek and powerful. She laps the pool again and again, in long, languid strokes that slice effortlessly through blue-black water. He marvels at her. He sips his whiskey. Ice cubes shift and clink in his glass. It is humid, late winter in Paraguay—the damp, immersive heat of the barber's towel, of evenings in jungle encampments and in the kitchens of childhood. On the edge of his vision, lightning bugs shimmer and weave in the twilight. He can hear the distant music and tinny laughter of a TV somewhere, the clatter of parrots in the trees, the puling of a ship's whistle on the river.

From out of the shadows, a guard steps in, salutes, approaches. And just like that, a spell is broken. He sends a message, a reminder about his engagement tonight. "Yeah, yeah," the *señor* snaps. "Go tell Gallardo." The guard salutes again, retreats.

The Presidente-in-Exile drains his whiskey. He must shower and shave and dress for dinner. But he pauses. In the *cañón* behind him, beyond the wrought-iron fence, he can hear the dogs scrabbling through thick brush. (Rottweilers, he's been told. Attack dogs trained not to bark.) Far above, the roar of an airliner approaches, crescendos, recedes. All around, the sudden thrum of bush crickets revving up like evening's engines. And the bug zappers, cerulean maws afloat in the enfolding dark, and the sputter and snap of their every tiny kill. And the slap of water and the delicious insuck of Dinorah's breath at the near turn, where the Presidente-in-Exile sits, his slender ankles crossed, shaking up the ice in his empty glass and secretly watching his mistress swim.

•

The Presidente-in-Exile is telling a dirty joke.

Two whores come to the handsome young priest for absolution. The priest invites them both into his tiny confessional. Sins are detailed, passions are stirred, and contortions ensue, followed by the sudden appearance of a guileless and comely young nun, and then the village idiot, who is hung like a bull. The Presidente-in-Exile is mucking up the joke, but his audience is a forgiving one: Aurelio and Méme on leave from the counterinsurgency back home; Lucho, in from Rio; and Luís and Humberto and Papa Chepe from Miami—some of the old *comandantes* down for a visit, in a private dining room at Bolsi, the toniest of Asunción's downtown restaurants.

The Presidente-in-Exile's joke careens brakeless down its narrative tracks, the confession stall impossibly stuffed with one character after another—concupiscent anarchy, a Marx Brothers porn flick. The *comandantes* bark and roar with laughter. They are tossing back carafes of wine, pounding the table and each other's backs. They are big men, and the cozy private room is a crush of humped backs and meaty forearms and big, ruddy faces. In the world of the joke, the *alcalde*'s virgin daughter has just entered the confessional. Papa Chepe runs out of the room and returns dragging the maître d'hôtel, a regal gray-haired woman in her fifties. The archbishop has now arrived for a surprise inspection, and Méme rushes into the kitchen, rousts a busboy, a Guaraní Indian who speaks no Spanish. Papa Chepe kisses the maître d' on the mouth and pushes her to the carpet. Méme shoves the busboy on top of her. The restaurant proprietor, accompanied by three male diners, enters to attempt a rescue of the maître d'. Papa Chepe pulls a pistol and puts the muzzle in the proprietor's mouth. The proprietor pisses his pants. Exit male diners. A vengeful pimp has arrived at the church and approaches the ruckus in the confessional, whereupon the proprietor is thrown to the carpet and compelled to gyrate at gunpoint against the busboy. Then the police arrive. Aurelio snatches Papa Chepe's gun and submerges it in a tureen of *bori-bori*. The police are nervous. Their captain approaches the Guest of Honor warily. But the Guest of Honor is in a good mood. He laughs and cajoles. He peels bills off a wrist-thick wad and moves through the cadre of cops, tucking the money into shirt pockets and cap bands. The police officers talk among themselves for a moment, then arrest the proprietor, close the restaurant, and post guards outside.

Lucho raids the bar, returns with bottles of Chivas and Rémy. The men drink, sated and suddenly quiet, pensive. Luís takes a pull and passes the bottle and begins to reminisce about his first skirmish, against coffee farmers in rebel territory. His story, of a green recruit, of a boy compelled by duty to become a man, has the rest of them nodding wistfully, until more stories come— liquor-stoked recollections of the bunkhouse and the whore-house, chronicles of love and war, and of the lusts of blood both literal and metaphoric. They regale each other with tall tales of jungle work and counterintel, and with anecdotes from the inter-rogation arts—stories of baseball bats and needle-nosed pliers and toilet bowls filled with excrement, stories of the light socket and the copper wire, of the salt and the wound, of the flesh and the spirit. Nostalgia like an emetic disgorges from them one dewy reminiscence after another until they are left weeping and hoarse, and Papa Chepe totters off the floor and caroms into the arms of the Presidente-in-Exile and tearfully kisses him on the lips. *"Maricones!"* Luís shouts. They all laugh. The Presidente-in-Exile stands up and speaks haltingly. He stammers something about family and comradeship, and discipline and duty, about his father and his legacy, and justice and reckoning and getting fucked in the ass by history. It goes around and around and then goes nowhere at all, and although it makes little sense, it is heartfelt. And so his men are moved. They cheer and curse and roil around their Presidente. They hoist him upon their shoulders and carry him about, and as they pass him across the threshold into the main dining floor, they whack his head on the lintel. Blood laces down his face and into his eyes, where it stings and mingles with his tears. For the Presidente-in-Exile is crying—a happy man, wobbly and unsteady upon the shoulders of his men, struggling for balance with one outstretched arm, and with the hand of the other pressed to his chest, attending to the barreling pulse of a damaged, brimming heart.

Two men meet at a newsstand in the lobby of the Hotel Méridien in Dakar. They greet each other effusively, hugging and kissing and clasping hands. *"T'as l'air super bien, mon ami!"* *"Non, non, c'est toi qui a l'air bien!"* They step outside, walk arm in arm. The plaza they cross hums and bustles on this clear and balmy late afternoon. City workers in white coveralls crawl all over a gigantic bronze statue of Lady Liberty astride a stallion in full gallop. They are festooning her with ribbons and garlands of green and yellow and red. Bunting streams from the spear she holds aloft. In the distance, the pock of fireworks. The city of Dakar anticipates a celebration—Senegal's Independence Day. April 4, 1980.

The two men order Nescafés at a makeshift bistro. In their brief stroll from the hotel—down a narrow street off the boulevard and into an arterial maze of dark alleys—the neighborhood has shifted from upscale to dicey. Alone, the men are much less effusive. In low and perfunctory tones, arrangements are made, and money changes hands—a fat manila envelope tucked into the folds of *Le Soleil*, pushed across the table.

Six weeks later, a freighter under Bahamian flag sails west from the Port of Dakar into the Atlantic, bound for Colombia and laden with phosphate ore, peanuts, cotton, millet, salted fish. Among its unregistered cargo: raw heroin, duffel bags of marijuana, and a small but heavy wooden crate labeled TRACTOR PARTS, containing sixteen Chinese B-50 rocket grenades, four Soviet RPG-7 launchers, and four boxes of percussion caps.

By mid-August, the crate sits unclaimed in a warehouse in Bogotá. One moonless evening two Lincoln Continentals filled with men arrive. Money changes hands—currency stacked, plastic-wrapped, and duct-taped into two tidy bricks. The crate is cracked open. Three launchers and twelve rockets are removed and transferred to the trunks of the vehicles. The rest is repackaged into a smaller crate, labeled HOSPITAL SUPPLIES. Some ancillary business is then transacted—two of the men are shot in the head, dismembered, and sealed into steel drums filled with used motor oil.

A week later, the crate is loaded onto a van and driven to a municipal airport in Quito, where it is relabeled TOOL & DIE and flown to Sucre. At the port of entry, a tightly rubber-banded wad of bills the size of a shotgun cartridge is slipped into the palm of a customs official. The crate is released and transferred onto a steam packet heading down the mighty, muddy Río Pilcomayo. It arrives in Asunción by the end of the month, in the last cool days of August, when the rains have subsided and the city has been washed clean for the last time. The crate is opened by three men and two women in the basement of a rented house on the corner of Avenida España and Calle America. It has been securely sealed, and with no pry bar they all struggle to get the box open, working methodically, quietly, so as not to alert the neighbors. They use screwdrivers and claw hammers, a fire poker, and the blade edge of a shovel. They lift out the rockets and the launcher and the percussion caps. They hug and kiss. They stash their booty in a crawl space behind the furnace and go upstairs and toast each other with cans of Bud and Coca-Cola. They drink to truth and beauty, to Marx and Darío, to justice and the death of tyrants. They put the hi-fi on low, mambo to Pérez Prado, slow dance to Iglesias. A bottle of rum has been pulled out, and Osvaldo plays bartender, pours drinks all around. He mixes a stiff one for Analisa. He will make the move on her tonight. She is three months pregnant, by Ramón, their *compa* just over the border in Argentina. But what the hell. She is incandescent tonight, flirtatious and shy, and Osvaldo is charming and clever. And these are auspicious times.

•

The Presidente-in-Exile is taking a leak.

It's a good one, the kind you remember for the rest of your life—a bladder dump, one of those butt-puckering gushers that makes the eyes flutter and elicits a rapturous "Ahhh!" The night is cool, and steam rises where he misses the wall he's aiming for. Where he doesn't miss, the cataract lays black washes onto the sand-colored stone. He chokes off, downshifts to intermittent trickles. He leans forward and settles his cheek onto the nubby granite wall, murmurs sweetly into the stone, "Fuck you." Over and over, like a lover's entreaty: "Fuck you fuck you fuck you . . ."

Gallardo waits a few yards away, beyond the hedgerow, pacing next to the Mercedes, which is parked at the curb on this quiet street. The entrance to the compound is on the main boulevard, up on Avenida Mariscal López. A twenty-foot-high stone wall topped with iron pikes runs along the length of the street. Gallardo paces, smoking a cigarette. He has just gotten the Presidente-in-Exile from Bolsi. No matter what, he was told, get me out of there before midnight. And they were heading home, until the *señor* directed him here. Gallardo hates this detour. It is embarrassing for him, having to explain to whoever may come upon them. For the most part, the guards here don't seem to mind, which puzzles him. But what if they come across a guard who does, some greenhorn coming at him with guns blazing? This is not how he wants to die, on lookout while his boss pees on U.S. property.

Gallardo sucks on his cigarette, drags deeply. Up ahead, a figure appears from around the corner, backlit by streetlights from Mariscal López. Gallardo watches the figure see him, see the car, watches the guard draw his M16 and move briskly toward him. He drops his butt and with his arms outstretched walks slowly toward the advancing guard, putting distance between him and the Mercedes. *"Está bien, está bien,"* he calls out. "Is okay." Although he still holds his arms wide, hands in plain view, Gallardo relaxes a bit. He recognizes this marine, this *negro americano.*

"Is okay." When he hears the voice, gets a better look at the car, the marine guard stands down. It's that tin-pot dictator, pissing in the bushes. He sighs, shoulders his weapon, greets the driver. "How you doing?" He takes a cigarette from behind his left ear, where he'd tucked it for this little break. "Is good, is good," the driver responds. The marine lights up, and the driver makes the international hand gestures for bumming a smoke. The marine gives him one, watches him slip it into a shirt pocket. "For later," the driver tells him. Both men hear a sharp metallic rapping. They turn to see the dictator finish pounding on the roof of the car and climb into the backseat. The driver rolls his eyes, smiles sheepishly.

The marine can't believe this shit is allowed. But the orders have been handed down, some unofficial understanding between nations: Let this fuck-wad piss on the United States Embassy. *"Vaya con Dios,"* the marine tells the driver. The driver returns the blessing, then says, "Yankee go home!" The marine laughs. He finishes his cigarette. He watches the Mercedes pull out and make a three-point turn and drive past him, back toward Avenida López. In the backseat, the ex-dictator is in shadow, but his head swivels as the vehicle moves past the embassy guard, who sends off our Presidente-in-Exile with the smartest salute he can muster and the precisely mouthed words: "Fuck you, too."


Standing in front of a hand mirror hung by a nail on the wall, Cook claws baby oil into her long black hair. She pulls and separates, creating three thick, lustrous cords. She plaits them tightly together, interweaving a long strip of bright orange muslin. She lays the braid over her left breast. No, the right one. Yes, better. She slips on a pair of soft black flats that she has spit polished with the inside hem of her skirt. She owns two pairs of shoes— sneakers for work, and these. Although Cook's ankles are thick

and sturdy, her feet splayed and rough-hewn, these shoes somehow render them fine-boned and delicate. She puts a pepper-
mint leaf into her mouth and crushes it. She slips her bag over
her shoulder. She exits her apartment—a single room, tiny and
spare and very clean—and leaves the villa grounds via the rear
service gate. She waves to the guard in the guard booth. He
waves back. She strolls a half mile down the road, to the *mercado*.
There is a coffee bar there, open late. She sits at the counter and
orders a *café con leche* and a biscotti. She pulls a *fotonovela* out of
her bag. It is entitled *Por un beso*, and relates the adventures of a
beautiful, innocent village girl in big, bad Mexico City. Because she cannot read Spanish, she gets most of the story line
from the actions depicted in the drawings. Cook gleans that
the heroine in the picture panels seems to triumph, that she
thwarts Lothario, and maintains Virtue, and gets a promotion
at her office job. As she reads, she looks up from the paperback
often, until—finally—her young friend Osvaldo pops in. He approaches her at the counter and smiles. *"Mba'éichapa nde pyhare,
Ynez."* Cook smiles back.

Cook's name is Ynez.

She has been with the villa for decades—sent to her great-
aunt when she was a child, and trained by her, taking over her
duties when the woman died. The owner of the villa is a Guaraní, and he has insisted that whoever leases his property must
also take the cook and the two Guaraní gardeners and the old
kennel master. Her whole life has been with the villa. Her
mother is dead, her father is old and blind and alone. She visits
him once a year up in the Gran Chaco, in a desolate village that
the young have abandoned. She sends him money each month.
He is grateful. "You are an ugly girl," he tells her, running his
chitinous palms gently over her face. "But you are a saintly girl."
And she has always believed this to be so. Until Osvaldo, who
gave her a second look one day. And whom she has run into in
this coffee bar two nights a week for the past month and a half.
And whose motives have always been transparent to her.

She doesn't care. Osvaldo is young and handsome, all toothy smiles and barrel-chested swagger. He is much too young to be flirting with such as her. But he does. She can see him looking for her when he enters, can see him light up and put on that smile and that swagger as he comes to her. Other women glance up at him, and they watch him come to her! He is not old and dull like the kennel master, whom she sleeps with occasionally— a kind man, but so diffident, and dull. Osvaldo is brash, voluble. He raises his voice, then brings it down to a growl. He flings his hands and arms about as he talks. His Guaraní is really quite good for a non-native, with the trace of an accent— Argentine, most likely. He is charming. He is loud and flashy, and asks too many questions. And then there is that wig—lopsided and shiny, and a shade of brown not found in nature, a wig that shouts WIG! to everyone. He is *so* obvious. She worries for him.

Osvaldo orders a *tereré*, with two straws. He sips, asks about her book, about the story it tells. He pushes the drink toward her and asks about her day with the *patrón*.

All her life she has kept her head down and worked hard, knowing or caring very little about the tenants of the villa: the Germans who stayed for more than a decade, quiet and monastic in their habits, until they left quite hurriedly one night; the university professors from Canada, hippie types who spoke Guaraní and insisted on eating only native cuisine; the Colombian, of whom she was very afraid and who lasted only a few months before Stroessner sent soldiers to put him on a plane out of the country.

And then the *patrón*. Since his arrival he was always going on about how awful Asunción was—a backwater infested with bugs and Indians, with shitty food and crooked cops and not one decent nightclub. She did not understand why a rich man who could live anywhere chose to live in a place he hated. Until Osvaldo explained to her that he had no choice. And in this way she learned about the *patrón*—his infamy, his fall, and his exile.

She takes a deep draw from Osvaldo's *tereré*. It is ice-cold, as is the custom. It hurts going down. She tells him about her day with the *patrón*, tells him about the luncheon she's expected to prepare tomorrow, after his return from a 9:00 a.m. meeting at the Banco Alemán downtown. She gives it all to him so he does not have to fish for the details. It is her gift to him.

She watches his eyes shift, sees them sharpen and glimmer for a moment as he takes in what she has just told him. And then he is Osvaldo again, brash and gay, slapping his palms on the counter, changing the subject. He tells her about a fender bender in front of his kiosk that morning, about the drivers who got out of their respective cars to confront each other. They were veterans of the Chaco War, old men in their seventies, wearing identical medals on their dark wool suits. They stumbled as they took swings at each other and missed, until—exhausted in the midday heat—they collapsed, and Osvaldo had to call an ambulance to haul them away. She loves how he regales in the telling of the incident, whether it happened or not. She is rapt, and hopes that her attention on him will keep him with her a bit longer. But she has given him what he's wanted. He glances at his watch, slaps his forehead. He remembers an urgent bit of business he must attend to, an errand for a cousin. And then, all showy and clownish, he brings Ynez's left hand to his mouth. She watches him kiss it. She feels suddenly bereft, lost. The floor beneath her seems to shift and sag. He bids her good night. *"Jajoecha peve, Ynez."*

*Until we meet again.*

And then he is gone.

The evening is clear and cool. The markets and shops have closed, and the cafés are putting up their chairs. The boulevard teems with late-night strollers slowly heading home. Cook joins them. Her route back to the villa is a riot of plumeria in full bloom. The air is glutted with fragrance. Sagging branches overhang sidewalks everywhere. Spatulate petals reach down fat and heavy into her face. She swats them away.

She waves to the guard in the guard booth. He waves back. Inside her apartment, she drops her bag and kicks off her shoes. She stares at a piece of honey cake wrapped in wax paper on the nightstand. She picks it up and goes outside. She walks to the iron fence that borders the *cañón* and kneels down. She squeezes the honey cake between her hands and waits. The kennel master has told her not to risk this, has warned her that his children are unpredictable, that they can be capricious and willful.

Soon the dogs come, pounding through brush, slamming into the fence, taking the cake from her. There is the snuffling of the dogs and the sound of their tongues on her, and then another noise, somebody speaking to her. She turns around. It is the *patrón*, barking at her in English. He stands there in his stocking feet, with his belt undone and a chicken leg in his hand. Here is the man who tossed handcuffed prisoners out of airplanes over the Pacific Ocean, the man who invented this innovation for disappearing dissidents. Here he stands, shouting about who knows what, wagging a chicken leg at her. She watches a trickle of blood thread down his forehead. An omen, she thinks. She gazes at him. She feels nothing. She will perhaps feel nothing for a long time. Except maybe for these dogs. She turns to them now, watches their fat pink tongues flicking out of the bushes between the iron pickets, rasping at her fingers and palms and doing a thorough job of cleaning her hands.

At dusk, the dogs are loosed. The sun dips below the ridge behind the villa, a photosensor engages an electric switch, and the kennel gate swings open. The two rottweilers set off separately, bounding over root and tree-fall and crashing through sedge and bramble until they join each other in a defile that cuts to the top of the ridge. They piss along the perimeter of the *cañón* fence, metal chain-link topped with boas of razor wire. They gallop back and forth along the ridge—lunging, tongue-lolling lopes. Paladino, the younger, harries Cerbero, nipping and snarling at him, always testing the older dog. They settle down and linger here in the waning light, splay-legged and slit-eyed and content, their massive skulls bobbing, their damp noses twitching at the verdant rankness of Asunción—acrid smoke from distant forest fires; musks of sewage and slag from the river, and eddies of sweet decay from landfills; ooze of meat from the slaughterhouse district; the complex admixtures of blossoms and bleach, baked bread and dog shit, mown grass and motor oil. And always, intermingled, the slick and slippery undertow of the collective human scent. Only when it is full-on dark—when the sun has dissolved like a tablet into the Pilcomayo, draining the colors from dusk—only then do they descend from the highest point of the property. Until first light, when they know to return to the kennel before the gates swing shut, the dogs have the run of this *cañón*. For the next eight or so hours they are free to romp and ramble and hunt and kill.

Guinea pigs are abundant year-round, as are lizards and toads. In summer, animals foraging for food and water come out of the jungle and down from the highlands. They breach the fence, attracted to the mulch of fallen fruit beneath the lime and papaya trees. Armadillos, capybaras, anacondas, a feral cat or two. Once, a tapir, far from its range, a two-hundred-pound calf that broke through and in a panic could not find its way out. It took them all night to chase it down. And once, there was a man, the greasy stink of him coming at them in torrents—the hot scent of prey like a desperate itching in the middle of the brain.

Once a week the master comes. He sweeps out the kennel, refreshes their bedding and their water trough. He brushes each of them, massages their hindquarters. Always Cerbero first. Paladino—patient—waits his turn. The master looks into their ears, checks their teeth, tends the occasional wound. He examines their droppings. He runs them through their commands. *Sit! Stay! Catch! Hold! Tear! Finish! Good boy!* When they are done, he kisses each of them. He is not afraid. The dogs know this. The scent of the master is neither of predator nor prey, of friend nor foe. He is simply the master. Before he leaves, he reaches into a waxed bag and throws a slab of round steak before each of them. The dogs watch him, mouths shut, eyes steady. On his command, they fall on the meat. They take food from no other.

But there *is* one other they are drawn to. She is redolent of blood, and deep in the fissures of canine memory lies a trace of what the tang of her blood once meant. (For Cerbero and Paladino are neutered males, and while the madness of the rut is absent, the absence is always present in them—dogs know their balls have been cut off.) It is this trace—the faint and fleeting residues of estrus and the mount—that brings them running. But they take food from her because it is the scent of the master that prevails. He whelms her, and she is steeped in him, and but for that, they would not come to her and gift her with their gentle mouthings. But for that, they would instead do all they could to clamp down on her hands and pull her in chunks through the *cañón* fence.


The Presidente-in-Exile is bleeding.

He holds a blood-dappled monogrammed hankie to his head. The cut is above the hairline, a tiny wound, but a real bleeder. He has just gotten home, flung his coat off, kicked off his pee-splashed Berluti mocs. He stands in front of the portable Sony in the kitchen, looking at a documentary—a history of the War of the Triple Alliance. In 1864, Francisco Solano López, third president of the Republic, invaded Brazil, then declared war on Argentina and Uruguay, engaging in a doomed six-year campaign that wiped out two-thirds of the population; by 1870 there were only thirty thousand men left in all of Paraguay. The debacle is rendered in history as a glorious act of national pride and will, and the ten-part documentary about it is aired on state television again and again. Aside from World Cup soccer in the summer and Miss Universe and the Oscars in the spring, television in Paraguay is a tedious déjà vu zone, awash in reruns of Stroessner's inaugural addresses and cooking shows from Argentina (*¡Mundo de bistec! ¡Barbacoa loco!*) and American sitcoms (*Hogan's Heroes, Green Acres, Happy Days*). And of course, the War of the Triple Fucking Alliance.

The Presidente-in-Exile sighs, flips off the TV. He cocks his head, listens. He drops the bloody hankie on a kitchen counter. He opens the refrigerator, finds a pair of baked chickens, and tugs at a drumstick until it comes off. He pads to the sliding glass door, unlocks and opens it, crosses to the iron fence a few yards away. He rat-a-tats the chicken leg between two pales, and waits. He knows the dogs are trained not to take food. They never come. But tonight he hears them, panting and tumbling down the hill, crashing through undergrowth, then moving past him along the fence perimeter toward the back of the house. Could they be hunting? He has heard that the dogs once killed and ate a man. Gallardo—talking to the gardeners or chatting up Stroessner's monkeys—has relayed such stories to him. A drug lord tossed an informant to them for vengeance and sport. A Mossad agent prowling for Nazis got trapped in the *cañón*. Some street kid climbed over the fence on a dare. The stories are varied; they always change, and they all intrigue the Presidente-in-Exile.

He follows the dogs along the gravel walkway that runs the length of the house for thirty yards, toward the back. Where the cook lives. He comes around the corner into a tiny patio area no more than fifteen feet square. A pool of light from Cook's open apartment door illuminates the soles of her feet, the backs of her calves. She is on her knees, up against the *cañón* fence. Her back is to him, and her hands are moving in the gaps between the iron pales.   .

The Presidente-in-Exile is peeved. She is feeding the dogs. "You're not supposed to do that," he says to her. He can see their tongues, pink and sudden at her hands in the dark. "Hey!" he says. "What the fuck are you doing?" She turns, and her level gaze confuses him. He looks at the chicken leg in his hand, points it at her. "You stop that *now*." But she doesn't. She seems unfazed, perhaps even bored. There was a time when he could have done anything to her and gotten away with it. There was a time when women were afraid of him. But he sees nothing in this *india*'s face. It is the face of a woman who wouldn't care what you did to her. She turns away, back to the dogs.

And as swiftly as it came, his anger is gone, dropping away like a stone off a precipice. He sighs, picks his way back down the gravel path toward the kitchen. He gnaws absently at his drumstick. His eye stings and he wipes at it. Blood. The cut has opened up again. Something in his stomach shifts and plops, and he grimaces. He'll need a bromo before bed, and the thought of this leaves him somehow disconsolate and vaguely depressed, and only adds to the chain of disappointments in this life of exile.

The Assassin of the Presidente-in-Exile gets the word. Osvaldo, calling from the magazine kiosk on Avenida España, repeats the go code into the phone: *"Blanco, blanco, blanco."* The Assassin of the Presidente-in-Exile loads a rocket into the launcher and sets a percussion cap. He hoists the launcher onto his shoulder and rests the barrel on the lip of the sill. Through the open window he trains the sight on a statue in a sliver of park across the street. He focuses on it—Francisco Solano López, killed at the glorious battle of Cerro Corá in 1870. He can hear Analisa warming up the Chevy pickup in the driveway outside. The engine rumbles precariously. They've had trouble with the throttle, and she revs it up. He can see Josias at the curb watching for the Mercedes, his M16 shielded by a topcoat draped over his wrist. He sees Lourdes across the street, minding a baby stroller filled with Browning 9mm pistols and an Ingram MAC-10.

He sees Josias wave, hears the truck ease down the length of the driveway, piston-slap rattle receding. Through the sight he watches the Mercedes glide into view. He lifts the barrel of the launcher off the sill and glides with it until the Mercedes is stopped short, blocked by Analisa in the Chevy. He seeks the trigger and finds it and nestles it into the crook of his index finger.

The Assassin of the Presidente-in-Exile inhales. He is suddenly taken with the clarity of the scene before him. What a beautiful morning! Sunshine pours into the street, filling it like a container. The Mercedes sits submerged in radiance, tense and gleaming in honeyed light, as if straining against the very weight of light itself. It shimmers within the crosshatched field of the launcher's reticle.

The Assassin of the Presidente-in-Exile exhales. The rocket fires and scoots waggle-tailed toward its target twenty yards away, slips into the armored Mercedes. The Mercedes levitates for an instant and disappears behind coils of black smoke. The Assassin of the Presidente-in-Exile drops the launcher, stands up, peels off his latex gloves. The sofa behind his station at the window smolders from the rocket exhaust. A black circle six feet across is seared into the wall; the paint in it bubbles and pops. He goes out the back door of the house, into the yard. He can hear the *ack-ack* of semiautomatic fire—Josias and Analisa and Lourdes emptying their weapons into the wreckage. He passes through a gate in the property fence that opens onto an alley, turns right onto Avenida Venezuela, and strolls to a bus stop at the corner. The crowd there is looking past him, gawking upward at a column of smoke rising thickly into the blue. He turns, gawks with them. He recalls something from a book he'd been reading, a history of the North American Indians, and he tries to remember what it was Sioux warriors told each other before going into battle. The bus pulls up, and he stands on line with the other commuters. He jingles the change in his pocket. He can hear the click and pop of pistol fire, benign in the distance.

The bodyguards in the Datsun have arrived. He pays the driver, moves into the press of standing passengers, situates himself near the back door. He pats the Browning pistol in his coat pocket and says a prayer for Josias and Analisa and the others—his *compas* for these past fifteen months.

And then it comes to him, and he smiles for remembering it. *Today is a good day to die.*


In the backseat of the Mercedes, the Presidente-in-Exile looks up from his paper.

The newspaper in his hands disappears, goes *poof!* like a magician's trick. His hands smoke and glow and burst into flames. The suit he is wearing vaporizes. His eyeballs explode, and his mouth fills with gasoline. The backseat of the Mercedes becomes an arena of transformation, the effulgent white-hot heart of a flame brighter than a hundred suns, a whirlpool of shrapnel and fire taking its passenger apart. Hands—gone! Yet there is the glide of silk on the fingertips. Eyes—no more! Yet before them hang the pale breasts of a first love, a girl from Stony Point, New York, named Amanda. The slide of gasoline on the tongue gives way to the textures of *pulque*, milky and sweet. There is the smell of Cohibas, of Tres Flores brilliantine. The scrape of a father's beard against skin, the slap of breakers on a shore like the beating of a giant's heart. The tug of an erection. Strokes and caresses. A pressing upon the chest like the vise grips of God. Gunfire in the distance. There is running, stumbling. There is falling. Free fall. And amid the onslaught of sensations without stimulus and memories without context, amid the random firing of synapses in a brain poaching inside its own skull, what is revealed and understood of a life in its last instant—as the Presidente-in-Exile looks up from his paper and mutters "Fuck me" when his driver's head disappears—what is understood is simply this: the transformative power of weaponry and surprise.

In the back patio of a trattoria three blocks away, an old man sits hunched over the morning paper laid out on the table before him, waiting for his espresso to cool. With his right hand he flips the pages of *El Diario*. With his left he holds the crown of a gray felt fedora and fans himself with the brim. He turns a page, peers at it. The fedora in his left hand stops moving. His breath catches, stops, begins again. He throws his hat on the page open before him. He looks around with histrionic furtiveness, in the manner of a lonely old man reveling in the melodrama of the moment. He sees mostly other lonely old men. One is tearing up a croissant and feeding the pieces to a tiny yellow dog in his lap. Two others sit staring down at a checkerboard between them.

He nudges the fedora aside, revealing a full-page ad with the headline DO YOU RECOGNIZE THIS MAN? There is a picture, a blowup of a passport photo from some twenty-five years ago, of a glowering, beetle-browed man with black slicked-back hair and a broad, neatly trimmed mustache. The hair is now chalk white, full and untended. The mustache is ragged, and the brows have thinned out. The face is tanned. The glower is gone.

The old man reaches for his demitasse and tosses back the espresso. He shudders, gleefully. He calls to the waiter, orders another, and a crème de cassis as well. The waiter looks him in the face, bows, departs. Nothing. The old man giggles. He ponders a delightful paradox of photo portraiture—the picture in the paper is an accurate likeness of himself a quarter century ago, but so much so that no one will recognize it as him today. Remarkable. *"Ausgezeichnet!"* he says aloud. He shudders again, claps his hands. His chair gives a sudden leap. He hears a muffled roar, feels movement in the ground beneath his feet. The other old men look past him, upward, and he turns, cranes his neck. Above the apartment building across the street, a column of thick black smoke jeweled with embers boils upward. The waiter arrives, sets the drinks down, stands and gapes with the others, all of them watching the smoke drape across the sky like a closing curtain. The old man squints, sniffs. He can smell diesel fuel, burning oil, the stink of molten rubber. And something else, something distant and familiar. He reaches for his crème de cassis, raises the glass, and carefully brings it to his lips. He pauses. Yes, of course—the smell of burning flesh. He sips the thick, sweet syrup. The liqueur is served neat here, to the brim in a warmed cordial glass, in the style called Martyr's Blood. And although still atremble with giddiness, the old man spills not a drop as he drinks to whoever has died today.

Meanwhile, back at the villa, a bony cat rasps its tongue at a congealing smear of mashed bug on the slate tiles of the west patio. A wind from nowhere disturbs the trees and a blossom-fall erupts, sending slant flurries across the grounds. Security cameras tucked high and low throughout the compound click and whir to each other. In the kitchen, Cook slathers chicken parts with mayo, dices tomatoes and onions, and puts water up to boil, going through the motions of preparing a luncheon that will not be served. And upstairs, in the master bedroom, the mistress Dinorah sleeps. Twenty years from now she will serve iced tea to fellow expats on the balcony of her modest condo in Coral Gables. She will regale them with the stories they want to hear, of her life with El Presidente—the palaces and the private jets, the fetes and the galas, stories of jewelry and couture and thousand-dollar bottles of wine, of weekends abroad and late, intimate dinners with movie stars. But she will keep to herself the details of their last shimmering days together, when the ardor of their love seemed to flower even in the ignominy of exile, when they swam and gamboled in lagoons under the stars and made love all night and toasted the dawn with champagne, the both of them—sated and spent—taken truly aback by the remarkable clarity of light at sunrise in Paraguay.

But for now she sleeps, deep and hard, unencumbered by knowledge or memory or dream. She sleeps like a dead man.

# Officers Weep

7 00 Block, First Street. Parking violation. Car blocking driveway. Citation issued. City Tow notified.

5700 Block, Central Boulevard. Public disturbance. Rowdy juveniles on interurban bus. Suspects flee before officers arrive.

400 Block, Sycamore Circle. Barking dog complaint. Attempts to shush dog unsuccessful. Citation left in owner's mailbox. Animal Control notified.

1300 Block, Harvest Avenue. Suspicious odor. Homeowner returning from extended trip reports a bad odor—a gas leak or "the smell of death." Officers investigate. Odor ascertained to be emanating from a neighbor's mimosa tree in unseasonal bloom. "The smell of life," officer [Shield #647] ponders aloud. Officers nod. Homeowner rolls eyes, nods politely.

3900 Block, Fairview Avenue. Shady Glen Retirement Apartments. Loud noise complaint. "What *kind* of noise?" officers ask. Complainant simply says it was "a loud report." "A gunshot?" officers query. "A scream? Explosion? *What?*" Complainant becomes adamant, shakes walnut cane in fisted hand: "It was a loud *report!*" Officers mutter, reach for batons, then relent. Officers report report.

700 Block, Sixth Street. Public disturbance. Kleen-Azza-Whistle Cleaners. Two women in fistfight over snakeskin vest. Each declares ownership of claim ticket found on floor by officers. In an inspired Solomonic moment, officer [Shield #647] waves pair of tailor's shears and proposes cutting vest in half. Approaching the contested garment, he slips its coveted skins between the forged blades. And thus is the true mother revealed!

3600 Block, Sunnyside Drive. Vandalism. Handball courts in Phoenix Park defaced. Spray-paint graffiti depicts intimate congress between a male and a female, a panoramic mural of heterosexual coupling that spans the entire length of the courts' front wall, its every detail rendered with a high degree of clinical accuracy. Officers gape. Minutes pass in slack-jawed silence, until officer [Shield #647] ascertains incipient boner. Officer horrified, desperately reroutes train of thought, briskly repositions his baton. Second officer [Shield #325] takes down Scene Report, feigns unawareness of her partner's tumescent plight, ponders the small blessings of womanhood. Vandalism reported to Parks & Rec Maintenance.

900 Block, Maple Road. Canine litter violation. Homeowner complains of dog feces on front lawn. Officers investigate, ascertain droppings are fresh, reconnoiter on foot. They walk abreast, eyes asquint and arms akimbo, their hands at rest among the ordnance of their utility belts: radio receiver, pepper spray, ammo pouch, handcuffs, keys and whistles, and change for the meter. Officers jingle like Santas. Their shoulders and hips move with the easy dip and roll of Classic Cop Swagger. "That business back there," she says, "with the snakeskin vest?" He grunts in acknowledgment, scanning

the scene for untoward canine activity. "I—I liked that." Her voice is hoarse, throaty, tentative, as he's never heard before. He nods, purses lips, nods some more. She nervously fingers butt of her service revolver. He briskly repositions his baton. A high color passes from one steely countenance to the other. Officers blush. Mid-swagger, elbows graze. And within that scant touch, the zap of a thousand stun guns. Up ahead, another steaming pile, whereupon poop trail turns cold. Officers terminate search, notify Animal Control.

9200 Block, Bonny Road. Vehicular burglary. Items stolen from pickup truck: a pair of work boots, a hard hat, and safety goggles, and   per victim's description—a cherry-red enameled Thaesselhaeffer Sidewinder chain saw, with an 8.5 horsepower, 2-stroke motor in a titanium alloy housing, 4-speed trigger clutch with auto-reverse, and the words DADDY's SWEET BITCH stenciled in flaming orange-yellow letters along the length of its 34-inch saw bar. Victim weeps. Officers take Scene Report, refer victim to Crisis Center.

5600 Block, Fairvale Avenue. Traffic stop. Illegal U-turn. Officer [Shield #325] approaches vehicle. Her stride longer than her legs can accommodate, she leans too much into each step, coming down hard on her heels, as if trudging through sand. As she returns to Patrol Unit, a lock of her hair—thin and drab, a lusterless, mousy brown—slips down and swings timidly across her left eye, across the left lens of her mirrored wraparounds. Officer tucks errant lock behind ear, secures it in place with a readjustment of duty cap. Her gestures are brisk and emphatic, as if she were quelling a desire to linger in the touch of her own hair. Officer [Shield #647] observes entire intimate sequence from his position behind wheel of Patrol Unit. Officer enthralled. Officer ascertains the potential encroachment of love, maybe, into his cautious and lonely life. Officer swallows hard.

700 Block, Willow Court. Dogs running loose. Pack of strays reported scavenging in neighborhood, turning over garbage

cans and compost boxes. Worried homeowner reports cat missing, chats up officers, queries if they like cats. "Yes, ma'am," officer [Shield #325] replies. "They are especially flavorful batter-fried." Officers crack up. Levity unappreciated. Officers notify Animal Control, hightail it out of there.

2200 Block, Cherry Orchard Way. Burglary. Three half-gallon cans of chain saw fuel stolen from open garage.

7800 Block, Frontage Boulevard at Highway 99. Vehicle accident and traffic obstruction. Semitrailer hydroplanes, overturns, spills cargo of southwestern housewares down Frontage Road West off-ramp. Officers redirect traffic and clear debris: shattered steer skulls; fleshy cactus chunks; the dung-colored shards of indeterminate earthenware; the mangled scrap of copper-plate Kokopellis and dream shamans; and actual, honest-to-God tumbleweeds rolling along the blacktop. "Tumbleweeds!" officer [Shield #325] exclaims. "Yee-haw!" Roundup commences, and her face gleams with exertion and sheer joy. Her stern little mouth elongates into goofy smile, teeth glinting like beach glass in the sun. As they divert traffic, officer ascertains being observed keenly. The watchful and intimate scrutiny makes her feel, for the first time in a long while, yearned for, desired. Officer [Shield #325] gets all goose-bumpy and flustered, and likes it. DPW Units arrive in their orange trucks, unload sundry orange accoutrements, erect signage: CAUTION, SLOW, OBSTRUCTION. Officers secure scene until State Patrol arrives, with their state jurisdiction and their shiny boots and their funny hats.

200 Block, Windjammer Court. Tall Ships Estates. Criminal trespass. One-armed solicitor selling magazine subscriptions in gated community. Forty-six-year-old suspect is embarrassed, despondent, angry, blames his bad luck on television, on fast food, on "the fucking Internet." Officers suggest cutting fast food some slack, then issue warning, escort suspect

to main gate, buy subscriptions to *Firearms Fancier* and *Enforcement Weekly*.

2200 Block, Orange Grove Road. Criminal trespass and vandalism. Winicki's World of Burlwood. Merchant returns from lunch to find furnishings—burlwood dining tables and wardrobes and credenzas, burlwood salad bowls and CD racks, burlwood tie caddies and napkin rings and cheese boards—ravaged. Officers assess scene, do math: Burlwood + Chain Saw = Woodcraft Apocalypse.

800 Block, Clearvale Street. Possible illegal entry. Complainant "senses a presence" upon returning home from yoga class. Officers investigate, ascertain opportunity to practice Cop Swagger, to kick things up a bit. Officer [Shield #325] pulls shoulders back, adds inch to height. Officer [Shield #647] sucks gut in, pulls oblique muscle. Search of premises yields nothing. "That's okay," complainant says. "It's gone now." Officers mutter, blame yoga.

300 Block, Galleon Court. Tall Ships Estates. Criminal trespass and public disturbance. One-armed magazine salesman kicking doors and threatening residents. Scuffle ensues. Officers sit on suspect, call for backup, ponder a cop koan: How do you cuff a one-armed man?

2600 Block, Bloom Road. Public disturbance. Two men in shouting match at Eugene's Tamale Temple. Customer complains of insect in refried beans. Employee claims it's parsley. Officers investigate. Dead spider ascertained in frijoles. "Well, it's not an insect," officer [Shield #325] declares. "Spiders are arachnids, you know." "They're also high in protein," officer [Shield #647] adds. Customer not amused. Argument escalates. Scuffle ensues. Officers take thirty-two-year-old male customer into custody, and—compliments of a grateful and politic Eugene—two Cha Cha Chicken Chimichangas and a Mucho Macho Nacho Plate to go.

6700 Block, Coast Highway. Officers go to beach. They park Patrol Unit at overlook, dig into chimichangas, chew thoughtfully, ponder view. The sky above is heavy and gray, a slab of concrete. The ocean chops fretfully beneath it, muddy green, frothy as old soup. Officer [Shield #647] loves how the two of them can be quiet together. There is *some* small talk: the upcoming POA ballots; Tasers, yea or nay; the K-9 Unit's dogfighting scandal. But mostly there is only the tick of the cooling engine, the distant whump of surf against shore, the radio crackling like a comfy fire. Officers sigh. Officer [Shield #647] gestures with chimichanga at vista before them. "There's a saying," he says. "How's it go—

*"Blue skies all day, officers gay.*
*If skies gray and clouds creep, officers weep."*

Officer [Shield #325] chews, nods, furrows her brow. "It's an *old* saying," he adds. "You know. *Happy* gay. Not *gay* gay." She laughs. He laughs, too. Relief fills Patrol Unit. A weight is lifted, a door eases open and swings wide. His right hand slips from steering wheel and alights, trembling, upon her left knee. Her breath catches, then begins again—steady, resolute. Officers swallow, park chimichangas carefully on dash. Officers turn one to the other. Suspect in backseat asks if they're done with those chimis, complains he's hungry, too, you know, complains that *some*body in Patrol Unit didn't get to eat his combo plate and can they guess who? Officers terminate break, split Mucho Macho Nachos three ways, transport suspect to Division for booking.

400 Block, Glenhaven Road. Criminal trespass and vandalism at construction site. Four pallets of eight-foot framing two-by-fours chain-sawed into a grand assortment of useless two- and four-foot one-by-fours. Officers walk scene, sniff air. Sawdust, gas fumes, chain oil. It is a pungent mix, complex and heady. Officers inhale deeply, go all woozy.

2600 Block, Frontage Boulevard at Highway 99. Injury accident. Soil subduction collapses shoulder of 44th Street on-ramp.

Three vehicles roll down embankment. Officers notify EMT and DOT Units, assist injured, secure scene. State Patrol pulls up, kills engine, emerges from Patrol Unit like starlet at movie premiere. State Patrol is starch-crisp and preternaturally perspiration-free. State Patrol thanks officers for their assistance, flashes horsey smile, tips dopey hat. Officers sit slouched on Patrol Unit, watch State Patrol strut about. "Prince of Freeways," officer [Shield #647] mutters. "Lord of Turnpikes," he says. Partner suggests that a more collegial relationship with State Patrol is called for. "King of the Road," he continues. "Ayatollah of the Asphalt." Officers giggle, get all silly, love that they can be silly. DPW Units swing by, offer wide range of orange gear and signage: SLOW, CAUTION, choice of SOIL SUBDUCTION or SUBDUCTED SHOULDER.

2200 Block, Felicity Court. Domestic disturbance. Man with golf club pounds on washing machine in garage. Woman in lawn chair applauds his every blow, whistles, barks like dog. Dogs next door whipped into frenzy by noise, bark like woman in lawn chair. Soapy water jets in jugular arcs from innards of crippled washer, streams down driveway, gurgles into gutter. Officers linger in Patrol Unit, assess scene, swiftly reach unspoken agreement, gun engine, hightail it out of there.

1000 Block, Clearview Terrace. Traffic obstruction. Sinkhole reported in street, measuring twenty-five feet across by four feet deep. Officers peer down hole, whistle. DPW Units flush restraint down crapper, go whole hog in establishing perimeter—orange barricades and flashers, orange arrowboards and signage, orange-garbed personnel braiding Reflect-O-Tape throughout scene like carnival light strings. Sinkhole perimeter is now a secure *and* festive perimeter. Officers clash with tableau, sent off to disperse rubberneckers: "Move along, folks, nothing to see here, move along."

2200 Block, Oak Street. Public intoxication and urination. Outside Ye Olde Liquor Shoppe. Sixty-four-year-old man taken into custody. During transport to Division, officer [Shield #325] confesses: "I've always wanted to say that. You know: 'Move along, nothing to see here.'"

5500 Block, Pleasant Avenue. Vandalism. Eighteen mailboxes destroyed along roadside, lopped neatly off their posts in a bout of mailbox baseball, but with chain saw instead of baseball bat. "Mailbox lumberjack," officer [Shield #325] muses aloud. Shot at whimsy misses mark. "Har-dee-har," complainant says. "Ha-fucking-ha." Officer [Shield #647] wonders aloud if somebody maybe put their crabby pants on today. Officer [Shield #325] adds if maybe they OD'd on their potty-mouth pills, too. Argument escalates. Scuffle ensues. Fifty-five-year-old male complainant taken into custody.

2200 Block, Felicity Court. Domestic disturbance. Woman wielding shovel hacks at wide-screen television set in driveway. Under canopy of tree in front yard, shirtless man sits on case of beer, pounding brewskies, watching woman, offering profane commentary. Above him, slung into limbs and branches, wet laundry drips heavily—hanged men left in the rain. Dogs next door yowl and bay. Officers cruise by, tap brakes, assess scene, nod assent, hightail it out of there.

2500 Block, Fairmount Street. Criminal trespass and vandalism. Spivak's House of Wicker. Wicker chewed and chopped chain-saw-style. Officers move silently into gray wicker haze, powdered with wicker dust, in awe of the sheer totality of wicker havoc.

1900 Block, Cypress Avenue. Illegal assembly. Demonstrators blocking access to public health clinic, refuse order to disperse. All available units dispatched for crowd control. Officers gathered at staging area, briefed on use-of-force policy, on arrest and intake procedures, then sicced on crowd. Officers stoked, fired up, ready to rhumba. Hand-to-hand maneuvers seemingly long forgotten—armlocks and choke holds, the supple choreography of baton work—all return facilely to muscle memory. Crowd control progresses smoothly. Officer [Shield #325] musses hair clobbering balky demonstrator. A scrawny little hank slips loose, nestles against her right cheek, framing the side of her face like an open parenthesis. A semaphore of possibility, officer [Shield #647] muses, spotting her while clobbering *his* balky demonstrator. Amid the tussle and heat of arrest and intake, she looks up, seeks him out, finds him. She smiles, waves shyly. From across the tactical field, he smiles, waves back, sticks out tongue. She is suddenly overcome, startled at how the sight of him affects her. It is not just love, or desire, but something profoundly less complex, as unadorned and simple as the Vehicle Code. Officer laughs, cries. Tearful and giddy, she whales on her demonstrator with what she realizes is joy in her heart. Demonstrators cuffed, processed, loaded onto County Transport Units. Assembly dispersed. Scene secured. Officers spent, pink and damp in the afterglow of crowd control. Cop Camaraderie ensues. Shirttails tucked, batons wiped down, cigarettes shared. Backs and butts slapped all around.

6700 Block, Coast Highway. Officers go to beach, park at overlook. Officers pooped, reposed. They do not speak. They sip double lattes, ponder view. A gash in the bruise-colored sky bleeds yellow. Sunshine leaks into the ocean, stains its surface with shimmering light. He looks over at her, notices a discoloration, a swelling on her left cheekbone. His hand reaches out, his fingers touch the wound, touch her. "You're hurt," he says. She smiles, whispers: "You should see the other guy." They park their double lattes on dash, slip off their sunglasses, avert their eyes. They screw their faces against the jagged harshness of an unpolarized world, slip sunglasses back on. His hands reach for hers, their fingers clasp and enmesh, roil and swarm at the fourth finger of her left hand. Officers tug and pull, remove and park ring on dash. He reaches for her. She leans toward him; it is like falling. Officers fall. Afterward, they linger over their coffee. Wedding ring on dash glints in the shifting light, harmless as a bottle cap or a shiny old button, something a bird might snatch up. Officers watch a ball of sunlight flare up at earth's edge like a direct hit. Officers assess scene, ascertain world to be beautiful.

2200 Block, Felicity Court. Domestic disturbance. Officers pull up, kill engine. They dawdle in Patrol Unit, fiddling with the mirrors and the radio, double-checking the parking brake. Officers sigh heavily, climb out, and assess scene. Garage door closed. Curtains in windows of home drawn. Officers walk up driveway, pick their way through the detritus of television set and washing machine. They knock on door, ring bell. No answer. Neighborhood quiet. Dogs next door quiet. Birds quiet. Everything, in fact, is quiet. The quiet of earplugs, of morgue duty, and of corridors at 3:00 a.m. The quiet before an alarm clock goes off. Officers backtrack down driveway, approach west side of house, move toward a gate in the fence that leads to backyard. They move gingerly across a saturated lawn, squishy beneath their feet. Soapy water oozes into the tracks they leave. Up ahead, against an exterior wall of house, a pile of freshly cut wood comes into view—one-by-four posts and whitewashed flatboards painted with black block letters. "LIFE" one of them reads. "MURDUR" reads another. Chain-sawed picket signs. Officers' napes prickle, butts clench in autonomic response. They thumb the release tabs on their holsters, move toward gate. They lift latch, ease gate open. Above them, the sky clears and the sun breaks. The shadow of a distant airplane skims over them, glides across the lawn, disappears. Officers enter backyard. The back fence sags forward. Trellises and plant stakes list at crazy angles. A brick barbecue sits crumpled atop its sunken hearth slab. The deck along the west side of the house is a corrugation of collapsed planking. It is as if the earth here simply gave up, shrugged, and dropped six feet. Officers move along periphery of sink-hole toward the sliding patio doors that open onto deck. Their panes are shattered. The ground glitters with peb-bles of safety glass. From within, cool air drifts out. And then they are hit, bowled over by a surge of vapors foul and thick—the redolence of mimosa clawing at their eyes and throats like some monstrous blossoming from some-where inside the house. And then the noises. First, a loud muffled report—the only way to describe it. Then, rising from the basement—or from someplace deeper still—the robust glissandos of a chain saw, its motor throttling up and down, laboring mightily. And within this an indeterminate overtone—the cadence of voices, urgent and shrill. Shouting, or laughing. Or screaming. Officers unholster service re-volvers, position themselves at either side of patio entry. They slip off their sunglasses, take this moment to let their eyes adjust to the dark inside. They look at each other. His eyes are dark brown, like coffee or good soil. Hers are gray, flat as lead except for the glint of a pearly chip in one iris. They do not speak. They love that they don't have to say anything. Instead they reach down, check ammo pouches for extra clips, wipe palms on duty trousers. Eyes adjusted, they draw and shoulder their weapons. They brace their wrists, release their safeties, silently count three, and take a breath. Whereupon officers cross threshold, enter home.

# Only Connect

Two men followed a third man up the street one night. His name was Bennett, and he had just left a party where the woman who'd invited him used him to flirt with somebody else. She worked with Bennett in the labs at the medical center. They were both researchers on the same projects, doing cutting-edge work in psychopharmacology, where the big bucks were. They made very good money, but her apartment was much nicer than his, and he wondered if she made more than he did. She lived on the northwest slope of Capitol Hill, in a secure building that was a hundred years old and meticulously restored. It had a lobby with thick, bloodred carpet and stamped copper panels on the ceiling, and a cage elevator that rattled and clanked pleasingly as it took you up. Her apartment had many windows, and they all looked out over Lake Union and the boats huddled in their slips, and at the Olympic range beyond. As the party progressed, dusk settled and you could watch the snow-drape on the mountains sparkle in the last light before sinking into shadows. You could watch the Space Needle brighten, shimmering and upright in the clear night. It was his first time in her apartment, and he liked it, the spectacular view and the tasteful and elegant minimalism of the decor, uncluttered and clean. He had hoped something would come of this invitation, that being invited by her might mean something. But she had a lot of friends, and the place was teeming with strangers. Bennett was born here, and although she had been hired less than a year ago, she knew more people than he ever did.

He had somehow ended up with her in a corner of her crowded kitchen. They were seated across from each other at a tiny breakfast table, and she was telling him about a trip she was planning over Christmas, a trek along the Inca Trail in Peru. He was asking her questions to keep the talk going, and she was answering them, when a man detached himself from a nearby clique, smiled briskly at Bennett, and leaned against the wall behind her, holding a beer bottle in his hands. Bennett recognized him. He was a popular barista at an espresso bar at the medical center. He was young, narrow and pale, with lank black hair that flopped into his eyes. He wore one of those expensive secondhand bowling shirts that you find in expensive secondhand clothing shops.

"I heard it's not so dangerous down there anymore," Bennett was saying to her. "Not like it used to be, I mean."

She shrugged. "It's dangerous everywhere."

"I suppose."

"It could be dangerous right here." She leaned forward, toward Bennett. "You never know where danger lurks."

He looked at her and smiled. When Bennett was confused, he smiled. Her eyes glimmered. She smiled back. She was playing with him.

"I could be in danger right now," she said. The barista behind her was grinning, picking at the label on his beer bottle, and Bennett realized that he was the one she was playing with.

Two women appeared and tugged her out of her chair and swept her away. The barista looked at Bennett, toasted him, and tipped his beer back. Bennett watched the cartilage in the barista's neck bob up and down. Then he got up and left.

He slammed the cage door shut and stabbed at the buttons. He would not be her go-between. He was no flirting conduit. "Fuck her," he said. He liked hearing the words. "Fuck that shit," he said, alone in the elevator that ticked like an old clock as it carried him down. He stepped outside into a cold autumn night. He couldn't quite remember where his car was. He had drunk several beers really fast, and he was still buzzed. He guessed uphill, so up he went, chanting "Fuck her" in cadence to his steps. He could see his breath in the air before him. Maybe it was the brisk night air, the bracing uphill trudge. Maybe it was the cathartic power of the F-word, spoken aloud, over and over. But soon he wasn't angry anymore, only embarrassed. He'd probably had six conversations with her in the past year, mostly work-related, and from them he had constructed the framework of a relationship and conjured the hope of something more. But between his conversations with her she had a life all her own and, before them, an entire history he was not a part of. You can't know anybody, not really, not in the brief overlaps of flimsy acquaintance, nor in any of the tenuous and fleeting opportunities for connection that we are afforded. It was a bleak little moment of clarity, but it was for Bennett a certainty he could find comfort in. He felt better, tramping the streets of the city he was born in, pondering opportunity and connection, gauging his prospects—the next disappointment, perhaps. Or maybe not. And suddenly he remembered where his car was parked—clarity begets clarity!—when a voice very close behind him asked: "Fuck who?"

Bennett turned around, and two men were on him, shoving him swiftly backward and crowding him into a gap of hedge and against the wall of a brick building.

"Wallet. Money. Now."

He looked at the one who spoke, a tall young man in a dark hooded sweatshirt, holding tight fistfuls of Bennett's jacket and pushing hard against Bennett's chest. He looked at the other man, who was shorter, and older. He wore a sport coat and slacks, and he was pressing a pistol into Bennett's belly. Bennett had never had a gun pointed at him before. He thought it would be bigger.

"So are you deaf or what?"

He looked back up at the man who'd said this, the younger one, the one without the gun. Shouldn't the one with the gun do the talking? Bennett was not deaf, but he wasn't sure which one to tell this to. He looked from one man to the other and back. The face of the younger one was an inch away from his. His breath was sweet, cloying and thick, like rotted candy. Bennett felt sick. He couldn't breathe.

"What are you going to do?" he gasped. "Shoot me?"

It was his most immediate concern, and a legitimate question, although maybe not the one you ask out loud. It was the wrong thing to say. Bennett was a little drunk, and suddenly very afraid, but also confused. So he smiled.

It was the wrong thing to do. The younger man loosened his grip. "Shoot him," he said.


So Costas shot him.

They were driving to Astoria, Costas and the kid, to get ahold of some methamphetamine. They had dipped into their buy money, splurging on rib eyes and dirty martinis at a Black Angus in Bellingham, and they needed to make that up. They pulled off the I-5 in Seattle, parked the car, and walked up this hill until a man came out of a building, and they followed him.

Every four weeks or so they made a run to Pasco or Yakima, or as far south as Ashland if they had to. But Astoria was their favorite. Yakima was touch and go these days. The town had gone all fancy and upscale with the winery boom. There were too many strangers, and the supply was not always steady. And Pasco was just a fucking chore. The Mexicans they dealt with were quarrelsome and ill-tempered. They enjoyed needling the kid—*maricón* this, *maricón* that—and got a kick out of it when he invariably flared up and Costas had to settle him down. But Astoria was steady and mellow. The connection in Astoria was *tranquilo*. They always looked forward to that run. Costas drove, and the kid would stuff the CD changer with Led Zeppelin, slapping John Bonham's drum work on the dashboard and screaming the lyrics out the open window into the rushing night. They pulled into rest stops, where they would do more lines, and the kid would go down on Costas, who hung on, knuckling handfuls of hair, bucking and groaning, and astonished still at the good fortune of this boy in his life.

They had met six months earlier when Costas went down to the carport one night and climbed into his car and started it up. He turned to back out and looked into the rear seat and saw this boy sleeping hard, dead to the world. It was a cold, damp spring, the usual in Bellingham, and Costas brought him inside and made him pancakes, and one thing led to another, and the boy stayed. Would it last another six months? Would it last through Christmas? What lasts, anyway? But it would do for now because that's what matters, after all—the Right Now. Money in your pocket and cocaine's rush and buzz, and this beautiful boy's head in your lap.

Astoria was their hideaway, their love nest, whatever you want to call it. They would stay an extra night or two at a Red Lion down along the river, where every room had a balcony with a view of the marina and the Astoria Bridge, a very narrow two-lane steel structure that shot high over the Columbia to the Washington side. In the evenings, when mist whirled and settled onto the water in the distance, the bridge seemed in its trajectory to fall short of the opposite bank and plunge into the river, a bridge to nowhere.

Some nights they drove across into Washington, to a seafood

restaurant in Chinook. It had once been an Episcopal church, and the nave was now the dining room, overlooked at one end by a stained-glass window of wooden ships on a storm-tossed sea. They ordered cioppino, and it came in a huge bowl with clams and mussels and crab parts sticking out. They put on bibs and used tiny tools to get at the meat and sopped up the broth with crusty bread. They lit up cigars and took a late-night stroll to walk off their meal. It was a small, narrow town, maybe five blocks wide, and made up mostly of vacation homes strung along a riverfront highway. Costas was a dog lover, and he kept kibble in his coat pockets to toss to the pooches that ran along the fences they walked by. Sometimes they set their lit cigars on the curb and stepped between the darkened houses, moving through open garages, peeking into the glove boxes of unlocked cars. Back doors were invariably unlocked, and they went inside just to see how easy it would be here, listening to the folks asleep in their rooms somewhere, and pocketing an insignificant trinket or two—a magnet off the refrigerator or a TV remote control—with only the dog of the house sniffing solemnly at Costas's pockets for more treats.

But usually they stayed in Astoria. They got a bottle of Hennessy and a bucket of fried chicken and lay in bed watching cable TV late into the morning. They smoked cigarettes on the balcony and flicked the butts into the water and watched the gulls fight over them. They went to a bar on the main drag that was underneath the bridge. The boy marveled, running back and forth, gawking overhead like a rube in the big city. A massive three-storied slab of concrete anchored the trussed roadway above, and he pressed himself against it and peered along its vertical surface up into the crossbeams and struts as if drawing a bead on the secret of bridges. Then he ran into the bar to report to Costas, who was playing liar's dice with the barkeep. Outside, then in again, tugging on Costas's sleeve like a child, nattering about smallness and bigness, and vastness and scale. "Bolts the size of your fist!" And then mile-by-mile replays of bridges he'd crossed—Pontchartrain in Louisiana, the Seven Mile Bridge in the Florida Keys, and one in the Chesapeake Bay that he swore to God dipped underwater and became a tunnel, then rose out to become a bridge again. And then in movies—the rope bridge quivering over a sheer ravine with a warlord hacking at one end of it, a bridge in Europe strapped with dynamite as Nazis swarmed across it, bridges that rattled apart in awesome earthquakes or got bent and twisted under the magnetic power of alien forces. He was jacked on coke and speed, wound tight and motormouthing, and so in and out, in and out, in and out, until the barkeep begged Costas—whom he knew from prison in Vacaville many years before—to please shut the boy up. "Put a leash on your pup, Costas!" And it was a good laugh for everybody, even the boy joining in with gulping, ratcheting hiccups of laughter. But back at the motel he wanted the gun so he could go shoot that fat fuck bartender in the mouth. Costas was rolling around in a tight ball on the carpet with his gun pocket underneath him, the boy kicking at his head and ribs. Then he tried for the car keys, but Costas got to them first, and the boy jumped up and down on Costas's fisted hand until the bones broke. Costas was tenacious. There was nothing you could do to him that had not been done to him before. And even as cranked as the boy was, he relented, heaving and exhausted, and settled for the wallet on the nightstand. He took all the cash and left. He turned up in Bellingham two weeks later, grimy and red-eyed. "Happy to see me?" the boy said, pushing past Costas into the apartment, glancing at the cast on his hand. He pulled off his clothes and headed for the bathroom, reeking of the street and of whatever he'd gotten into. "What, you gonna cry?" he said, watching Costas watch him, standing naked in the steam and letting the hot water run, then stepping into the shower stall.

*Inconstant moon.* Costas didn't remember where he'd heard that, but that's what the boy was. One day, he would not come back. So the boy showers, and grateful for his return, Costas cries. He is enthralled, and he knows it. Would he do anything for this boy? Well, no. Not anything. But okay, he might. All right. Yes. He would.

*Shoot him.*

So Costas shot him. The gun was small and didn't make much noise, two benign pops, like the rap of a knuckle on window glass or the click-crack of a walnut being opened. Costas hated the gangbangers with their huge pieces and all their stopping-power bullshit. Up close, a .22 stopped you just fine. He shot him twice in the belly and put the gun away, and they both eased him onto the ground. The man was watching them go through his pockets. Then he said a woman's name and closed his eyes. They got around sixty dollars, plus ATM and credit cards. The cash would cover them tonight, and they knew somebody who'd pay a hundred dollars for each card.

They took two steps out of the hedge and another step over a grassy strip and stood on the sidewalk nose to nose with a woman staring at them. She was a chubby, moonfaced girl, all big-eyed and O-mouthed. She dropped a small paper bag that hit the pavement with a tiny thud, then rolled in a half circle and began to wigwag down the hill. The kid retrieved it before it got away. He opened the bag and peered inside. He pulled off his hoodie and looked into the woman's face and smiled. "Chunky Monkey!"

"C'mon," Costas said. "Shake a leg."

The kid rewrapped the bag carefully and held it out to her. She took it. "Thank you," she whispered. He flipped his hoodie back up, and they walked past her and loped down the hill.

"What's the matter with you?" Costas said, and the kid only grinned. She had gotten a good look at his face, and he didn't even care. Costas thought a moment: if, when he turned around, she was still standing up there goggling at them, then he would trot back and pop her. But when he looked, she was gone. All the better. They needed to get to Astoria. Their buy was going down and they could not dillydally.

When she got home, she dumped the ice cream down the sink and crawled into bed in the clothes she was wearing. She lay there listening to sirens in the night, to jets passing over on approach to the airport, to the drunks stumbling home from the bars on Capitol Hill. She heard the birds at sunrise and the garbage trucks wheezing up the streets. When it was light, she got up and used the phone. She left a message at work, then changed her clothes and went outside. It was a clear and cold fall morning, and she had her down jacket on. She could see her breath in the air. She walked three blocks and spotted a patrol car parked across an intersection just ahead. The street behind it was cluttered with more cars—blue-and-whites and unmarked sedans and a gray, windowless van up on the sidewalk. She asked the policeman sitting on his car what happened. He said nothing happened and told her to go on to work. "I called in sick," she said. "I'm not going to work today." The cop stared at her until she walked away. She tended to be overly thorough in conversation in a way that made her seem insolent or flip. She tried too hard, believing that being as precise as possible about what you thought and felt was how you connected with people.

That afternoon she read in the paper that somebody had been shot and killed. She sat at a small dining table in the kitchenette, drinking a medicinal tea. Because she had called in sick, she now felt sick. She lived in a basement apartment, and feet went by in the slot window above her dining nook—people coming home from work, footsteps and voices approaching and receding, approaching and receding. The man had let her get a good look at him. He had pulled back his hood and smiled into her face. He held her ice cream out to her. She took it. She thanked him. *I should be dead.* This is what she was thinking when she ran home last night and as she lay in her bed until the sun came up. This is what she was thinking now, running her hand across the newspaper spread on the table, smoothing it out. She believed she would never forget his face. She believed it would be sliced into her memory forever.

*I should be dead. But I'm not.*

She called in sick the next day, and the day after that. Maybe he was out there, looking for her. She stayed home and indulged in fearful fantasy. She peeked out her window at the steps that led down to her door. She jumped when the mail dropped through her mail slot. She gazed anxiously at the phone, which did not ring. She drank tea and dozed fitfully through the day, awaking at dusk to her darkened apartment. She kept the radio turned off. She did not need to hear about what had happened. A man was dead, and his killer was out there. She imagined staying in her apartment forever—the Woman Downstairs. But the romance of her fear soon dissipated, and she grew restless and bored and ran out of tea, and after three days she went back to work.

Her name was Hailey, and she was a paralegal assistant at a successful real estate practice. Long ago, in her first months out of paralegal school, they'd had a Christmas party where one of the lawyers she worked for had taken her into an empty office and kissed her for ten full minutes. He was twice her age and married, with three children in college. After the holidays he'd taken her to lunch and apologized, all stammering and shy. She hoped he would call this week, ask after her, wonder where she'd been for three days. But he didn't. She was twenty-nine years old, on the brink of her next decade, and in love with a man who did not call her after she saw somebody die.

She never told anyone. She moved gingerly through the weeks and months that followed, as if stepping from foothold to foothold to balance the secret she carried inside, the thing that no one could know. She was different now. Words no longer came tumbling out of her mouth, rushing to fill a silence she once dreaded. She was contained, withheld. At first she had felt guilty, had been laden and bleary with it, and people at work had asked if she was all right—even her lawyer. But the guilt lifted quickly, and then she felt guilty about that, until that went, too, and soon she felt only clean and new and grateful, as if, climbing out of bed from a long and frightening illness, she now stood blinking in bright, clean light. She felt lucky. She was alive.

Years passed. Hailey waited for her lawyer. She watched him grow old, divorce, marry again. Then he died, and she was alone once more. His son stepped into his father's shoes at the firm and treated Hailey with kindness and respect. She was an esteemed figure in paralegal. "My father always liked you," he told her. And she thought: *So he did remember.*

She moved north, across the canal to Green Lake, and every evening, rain or shine, she walked the path around the lake in the park. She had seen other old women walk the lake, striding briskly past, all vital and vibrant, nodding and saluting at everybody. Who were these fast walkers, these show-offs? Where were they going so fast? Hailey was in no hurry. She kicked through swaths of fallen leaves. She sloshed into deep puddles in her waterproof boots. She stood in downpours to watch red-winged blackbirds flit crazily through the reeds along the bank, or to follow the progress of an intrepid swimmer cutting the rain-pocked surface of the water. She stopped for shaved ice at the snack shack, gave her change to the regular panhandlers, sat in evening's last light watching the kids on the monkey bars. Mothers smiled solicitously at her and she smiled back. Near the small boat launch she peered at a map of the park and eavesdropped on boys and girls on first dates teasing and cajoling each other into rowboats. She spotted a walking stick once, a slash of green against a brown thicket, and she stopped for an hour, drawing a small crowd that joined her to observe the insect step gravely along a narrow twig. Hailey was alone, still. She had never even gotten a pet, neither dog nor cat nor bird. Pets were substitute companions, and she would have a real one or none at all. She had read somewhere, long ago, that solitude was not a sad thing, but a vital and transformative phase, in preparation for love. She didn't believe it anymore. But she still remembered it.

One day at work, Hailey was going over preliminaries with a client entering into a commercial leasing arrangement with her son-in-law. She was a silver-haired woman who sat regal and straight-backed in a chair across from Hailey, who was taking notes. She was saying that she loved her daughter, but did not like or trust the man she had married. She called him a heel, and an ass. She was from the South, and when she spoke, she elongated these words into two syllables: *hee-uhl*, *aa-uhs*. She was saying that she wanted the legal arrangement to be rock solid and unimpeachable, to protect herself and her daughter from certain ruin. She stopped talking mid-sentence. Hailey looked up from her notes. The woman was crying.

Hailey capped her pen and took off her reading glasses. She looked from the woman's face to the window behind her, and the woman turned in her chair to look as well. They sat in a conference room on the nineteenth floor of a building downtown, and through the plate-glass windows they had a spectacular view of the bay. It was late afternoon, the end of a hectic week, and the office was still. Outside, gray clouds hung in panels across the sky, and the light moved behind them. The water changed color from blue to green to silver. Shafts of light tilted down from nowhere and tracked the surface and disappeared. Tiny ferries docked and departed. Finger-size cargo ships slipped seaward. The conference room grew bright and dim, bright and dim— the vast and languid heartbeat of sunlight itself. The woman reached a hand out behind her, and Hailey looked at it for only a moment and reached across the table and took it, and she did not let go.

She did forget his face. Everything fades. Everything goes. Long after the woman she loved had died—after brief, good years that Hailey thought she'd never have with anyone—there were moments when he would come back to her. A cold fall night, the sweet rot of dead leaves, the thrum of far traffic in a city's teeming silence—these would bring him back, not like a photograph, but rather the memory of one, as if someone were describing his photograph to you, and you listen and think: *Oh, yes.* His smile was sweet and taunting. He held the bag out to her, daring her. And Hailey—long ago, on a Saturday night ice-cream run—reached out and took it from him and thanked him, and meant it. She was alive.

# Temporary Stories

Ine day, early in her life as a temporary employee, the Agency called with a new assignment for Clarissa Snow. It was a long-term job, eight to twelve weeks. But it was phone work, and Clarissa Snow was not a phone person. "We *know* that, of course," said Mrs. Delahanty, her Placement Counselor at the Agency. "But we're in a pickle with this one, and we could sure use your help! You're our best girl. You know that, don't you?" She did know that. "And you can say no if you want," Mrs. D. told her. "You know that, too, don't you?" She knew that, too. But she also knew never to say no to an assignment. For while the mechanisms of temporary employment were a black box to her, its laws were simple and unforgiving. If you ever said no, you never worked again.

A receptionist in the Human Resources Office of the county hospital had quit without notice, and they needed someone to fill in. On Clarissa Snow's first day, the other receptionist went over the Human Resources Office phone protocol: Always answer before the third ring; always answer with either "Good morning!" or "Good afternoon!" followed by the institution name, the office name, your name, a brief pause, and then "How may I help you?"; always ask the caller's permission before putting the caller on hold; never keep the caller on hold for more than two minutes; after two minutes, always check back to ask if the caller minds being on hold; and so on. The other receptionist ticked off each procedure on her fingers while Clarissa Snow took notes. The other receptionist was a very large woman who confided to everyone, without anyone's asking, that her largeness did not bother her. "Yes, I'm fat!" were the first words she said to Clarissa Snow. "And proud of it!" she added proudly. She took the phone protocol very seriously and spoke of it with meaningful pauses to convey that seriousness. "We are," she said, "representatives— . . . of this institution. We provide— . . . service. And that— . . . is our mission." Clarissa Snow nodded. "Representatives," she wrote in her notepad. "Mission," she added, and then, in double underline, "Service."

The two of them worked in the Human Resources lobby, within a circular counter situated in the middle of a low-ceilinged, windowless room with recessed fluorescent lighting, dusty potted plants, and the oil portraits of hospital benefactors bolted to its walls. There were twenty-one chairs arranged in three semicircular rows facing one quadrant of the counter, and twenty-one clipboards with twenty-one pens attached to them by twenty-one tiny chains. And every day, from eight to five, there were twenty-one applicants rocking and fidgeting in these chairs, filling out job forms. Upon this beige-carpeted sea of employment anxiety, the other receptionist captained an efficient little ship of mission and service, gliding from computer to printer, from fax machine to phone console in her wheeled chair, which she steered expertly with her tiny feet. She could complete any task and offer any assistance without ever getting out of this chair. She could answer any question put to her and never move faster than was *just* necessary for whatever crisis was at hand. Clarissa Snow often caught herself staring in open-mouthed awe at this woman, who spun chaos into order while turning placidly within her circular domain. She was like a twister in reverse, gliding cows into their pastures and floating roofs down upon houses.

There were eight phone lines at the reception desk, and they never stopped ringing, and Clarissa Snow's job was to answer them. On her first day, she said "I don't know" to so many callers that the other receptionist referred to her as the I Don't Know Girl. "Just give them to me," she said gaily. "Just give them all to me until you get the hang." And as the morning progressed, so did Clarissa Snow. For some questions she consulted the Learned One, the other receptionist's pet name for the Employment Bulletin, a black, half-foot-thick duct-taped ring binder of job listings for the entire county hospital system. Handling these calls was as easy as looking up a word in a dictionary and reading a definition into the phone. For questions that the Learned One could not handle and the I Don't Know Girl could not yet possibly know—which schools offered EMT certification, for instance; or whether they would be hiring occupational therapists in the near future; or what the lunch special in the cafeteria was—for these questions, Clarissa Snow put the callers on hold, for no longer than two minutes, and gave them to the other receptionist, who—while simultaneously coding an applicant's job forms or proofreading copy hot off the fax machine—took each call in turn, nodded with equal gravity to each query, and answered immediately: Northpoint College, possibly next month, and Cajun chicken with garlic mashed potatoes. Clarissa Snow noted the correct answers and eventually got the hang of these calls as well. "My, my," the other receptionist said to her just before the lunch hour. "We'll need to find another nickname for you, won't we?" Clarissa Snow beamed as she left the lobby for lunch. The benefactors on the wall—a high gloss in their pink cheeks—seemed to beam after her.

O hubris of the temporary employee! For that very after-noon Clarissa Snow received a series of phone calls for which she was completely unprepared. "So," began a woman on Line Six. "Do *you* think I should apply for this position to get my foot in the door and take the chance of getting stuck in a dead-end job? Or should I risk waiting for the job I *really* want to come up, which could possibly be never?" "Tell me," Line Three implored. "Tell me I haven't missed the application deadline for the job in Medical Records. *Please, please, please. Please* tell me that." "Guess where I'm sleeping," Line Four began. "Okay, I'll tell you. I'm sleeping on my brother-in-law's living room sofa. I'm a forty-four-year-old man sleeping on my brother-in-law's living room sofa, and if I don't get a job by the end of the month, the punk is going to toss me out on my ass." "I see," Clarissa Snow said. (What else *could* she say?) She was, by the end of the day, distressed and befuddled. But the other receptionist was encouraging. "A *good* day's work," she told her as they locked the lobby doors. And Clarissa Snow was comforted.

The next day was worse. One caller with questions about openings in Occupational Therapy proceeded to tell her about his messy divorce from "that bitch." (Later that week, a woman would call and discuss her divorce from "that bastard," leaving Clarissa Snow to ponder the coincidence.) A woman calling from a pay phone near some sort of major traffic artery shouted absurdly generic questions about employment—"What kind of work do you have! How much do you pay!"—then abruptly asked if you had to skip a meal, which one would you skip? An ex-priest struggling to get back into the job market confessed, with quivering voice, that he was scared. And there were more such as these, caller after caller who took Clarissa Snow's rote offer of help and service too readily to heart; who begged her for work and pumped her for advice; who shared more than she needed or wanted to know about themselves, and without warn-ing sent her sprawling into the intimate muck of their lives, clutching at her simply because she was the one who picked up the phone.

The other receptionist, of course, handled these calls expertly. She had an answer for everyone. Platitudes bubbled out of her as if from a ceaseless wellspring of benign concern. "That field is *very* promising. And that kind of work can't be replaced by a machine, you know." Or, "Well, breakfast *is* the most important meal of the day. Breakfast is definitely a keeper." Or, "These *are* difficult times, darn it! But try back in the spring. Things *always* come up in the spring!" She nodded appreciatively, uh-huhed understandingly, then blissfully reeled off whatever cliché popped into her head.

By the end of her second day, Clarissa Snow had the jitters. And by the end of Week One of her eight-to-twelve-week assignment, she had developed an eczema rash on her neck and arms. She was popping aspirin like breath mints. Her hands would not stop shaking. Her bus ride to work in the mornings felt like the Bus Ride of Doom, her mind racing in loops of dread of the day to come. And out of this heat of her frenzied anxiety came the Jobless Beast, the coalescence of all callers: a large, sad, hulking thing that lived only to forage for employment; that slept in its car under freeways at night and emerged by day to make calls from pay phones; that loped from Human Resources Office to Human Resources Office, presenting itself with an awkward smile and a jocular tone edged with desperation, stooped and cramped from its hunger for work, for any morsel or crumb that Clarissa Snow had to offer, crying out to her, I'll do anything, I'll do anything, just help me, please. Why me? Why me? she implored the Beast in her mind. Because, the Beast implored back, because you answer the phone.

Her lunch hours, once easeful respites from the office, were now taken up with escape maneuvers from the Beast. She trekked as far from the hospital grounds as possible, hoping the malign presence of the Jobless Beast would diminish. It did, a little. She found scant relief at whatever bench or stoop would accommodate her, where she managed to eat her lunch: several raw brussels sprouts, a slice of apple on a bagel, a fistful of toasted soy nuts. An hour later she was back at her station behind the phone console. And after just a few calls her gut would begin to fill with a sadness so bloating that whatever she had managed to get down her throat at lunch would come right back up by afternoon break. As she dashed for the bathroom, the hospital benefactors regarded her from their ornate, theft-proof frames with undisguised pity.

Midway into Week Two, Clarissa Snow had spoken to a lonely retiree looking for part-time clerical work—"*Any*thing!" he laughed—who kept her on the phone for twenty minutes; to a recently laid-off medical transcriptionist whose wrist tendons had been surgically severed to alleviate her pain; and to a man who wept that he had been looking for a job for two and a half years. "I'm sorry," Clarissa Snow began whispering into her mouthpiece, "but I *can't* help you. I'm just the receptionist." At which point many of her callers said, "Let me talk to the other one, then." They did this so frequently that the other receptionist had a little chat with her.

"How do you do it?" Clarissa Snow pleaded. "How do you talk to them? *No*body can help these people."

"But they have no one else to call," the other receptionist said. And then, more firmly: "We— . . . are the department of last resort. This— . . . is Human Resources." Clarissa Snow nodded wearily. "Human Resources," she wrote in her notepad. And under that, "Last Resort."

For the rest of that morning Clarissa Snow made a fragile alliance with the tenets of mission and service that her job demanded. "Well, military service may be a viable job option," she told one caller, "but is it the option for *you*?" "No," she told another, "I don't think a second opinion is *always* necessary, although it can *sometimes* be necessary." "Yes," she agreed with another, "divorce *is* a tough row to hoe, isn't it?" For a while at least, she was getting the hang. It did not last.

"Can you help me?" Line Two said. "Because, you see, I'm at my wit's end here." It was a woman's voice, flat and uninflected. It came from a pure, dead silence, without background noise of any kind, and it gripped Clarissa Snow's innards like a fist. "So I was wondering," the voice continued. "I was wondering if you could help me. Because, you see, you're my last hope." Clarissa Snow shuddered. The buttons on the phone console winked at her. She quietly slipped the handset into its cradle and told the other receptionist that she was leaving a little early for lunch.

Outside, it was high noon in midsummer. The air was thick, and you could see the heat moving through it, rising visibly off the pavement, corrugating everything in the distance, and lending to the concrete-and-steel permanence of high-rises and overpasses a disconcerting waviness. It was a sweltering day, an unbearable day, but a day borne nonetheless. Lunchtime throngs swarmed the sunlit streets in search of food. Clarissa Snow zigged and zagged among them.

From a pay phone in front of a mini-mart four blocks away, she called her Placement Counselor. While on hold, she pulled out a cigarette; she'd started smoking again. Her hand shook as she lit it. "Now, now," Mrs. D. told her when she came on the line. "I want you to get a grip. Get a grip and tell me all about it." Clarissa Snow begged for a new assignment—anything, any-where, she didn't care. "Why, of course, dear," Mrs. D. said. "I can do that. I can do that for you. But you see—" And from the modulations and pauses in Mrs. D.'s voice, Clarissa Snow knew that she, too, was lighting a cigarette, pausing now to draw the smoke into her lungs. Clarissa Snow inhaled with her. "You see, that puts us in quite a pickle." She was their best girl, Mrs. D. said, their cream of the cream, and what would it look like if their cream of the cream curdled on an assignment? Then she wouldn't be their best girl anymore, would she? No, Clarissa Snow had to agree, she sure wouldn't. She dropped her cigarette on the ground and stepped on it. She thanked Mrs. D. for the pep talk and hung up.

A bank of tall, narrow trees stood along the edge of the mini-mart parking lot. Their topmost leaves shimmered in the sun, and Clarissa Snow—for sheer want of knowing what to do next—stood peering up at them as if they were her last hope. She then searched her bag for another coin, dropped it into the pay phone, and made another call. She was briefly put on hold. And when the other receptionist thanked her for holding and asked how she might help her, Clarissa Snow told her everything.

II.

Autumn in the city was crisp and clear and bright. It was a time of year when the windows in the high-rises flamed yellow-gold and the sunlight burnished every reflective surface to a painful gloss: the marble columns and cornices of building exteriors, trolley wires and turnstiles and door pulls, the brass filigrees on handrails and drinking fountains and trash receptacles. Windshields of passing vehicles flashed like gunfire, and broken bottles glittered in the street. The air was scattered with needles of light that made Clarissa Snow squint.

She was sent on a four-week assignment to an insurance company. Her job was to type and edit a Secret Report for the Executive Vice President, and this was her routine. At 8:00 a.m. she took the elevator to the Claims Unit on the twelfth floor and unlocked the door to an office that had been converted to file storage. Sagging boxes filled the room, leaning in precarious columns against the walls and each other. Just enough space remained for a desk and chair and computer and printer. She spent the day typing and revising and editing the Secret Report, and at 5:00 p.m. she delivered a computer disk and a manila envelope with her revisions to the Executive Vice President's Assistant on the twenty-ninth floor. Between 5:00 p.m. that day and 8:00 a.m. the next morning, *some*one would slip an envelope with new copy and revisions under the door of her office.

The Executive Vice President's Assistant was a tiny, no-nonsense woman, impeccably attired and of indeterminate youthfulness; she looked like a dour little girl playing dress-up for the day. She instructed Clarissa Snow not to socialize with anyone on the twelfth floor. "I've memoed them to not talk to you," she said. "Eat lunch alone," she told her. "Take your breaks outside the building or in your office. Keep your door locked. This is a *Secret* Report. That's why we hired an outsider for the job." She placed one of her perfect miniature hands—pallid and smooth—upon one of Clarissa Snow's, which by comparison seemed a vast, bony landscape of knuckle and joint. "The Agency says you're their best girl," the Executive Vice President's Assistant said. "So we're counting on you." Clarissa Snow nodded conspiratorially. She was thrilled with the secrecy. It excited her.

Although no one on the twelfth floor was supposed to talk to Clarissa Snow, adherence to this directive broke down quickly. During Week One of her assignment, Claims Unit employees winked at her in the elevator and put their index fingers to their lips in gestures of complicity. After one of the Claims Analysts mouthed a silent "Good morning!" to her in the ladies' restroom, other employees began to greet her in hushed tones. "How are you!" they whispered. "Fine! Thank you!" Clarissa Snow whispered back. Soon the Claims Unit Manager was knocking on her door, inviting her to potlucks in the lunchroom. "We know you're not supposed to," he'd say, then, looking up and down the hallway and dropping his voice, add, "Do it anyway!" He was an affable, red-faced man who wore wide, ugly ties, but wore them with irony; there was an ongoing contest among the men in his unit for who could wear the ugliest ties. The Claims Unit employees held birthday parties and years-of-service celebrations and maternity leave bon voyages on a regular basis, and they invited her to all of them. When she didn't show up, they came looking for her, knocking urgently at her door: "Are you all right in there?" They were kind and solicitous, eager to make her a part of things, and Clarissa Snow wanted none of it. She did not want to partake of their lives. She attended their gatherings under duress, making a brief appearance before returning to her Secret Report, often laden with paper plates of macaroni salad or potatoes au gratin. But for the most part, they left her alone. They did not take her aloofness personally.

Clarissa Snow was an extraordinary typist and often finished her work well before 5:00 p.m. On these days, she spell-checked the Secret Report, proofread it two or three times, then spent the rest of the afternoon thumbing through magazines she had smuggled in her bag. Her interests were varied and sundry, and wholly vicarious. Because she was afraid of flying, she bought travel magazines, wherein she browsed the pictures of exotic lands she would never visit. She read gourmet magazines, as she did not cook; gardening magazines, as she had no garden; dog- and cat-breeding journals, because her apartment building did not allow pets.

When she was done with her magazines, she stared out the window. She'd heaved some file boxes out of the way and discovered a floor-to-ceiling panel of tinted shatterproof glass. It gave her an unobstructed view of the high-rises across the street, and the high-rises beyond them, and the dim yellow mist that obscured everything in the distance. When this bored her, she snooped around. A narrow linoleum trail wended its way through the file boxes, which were labeled by fiscal year—FY72–73, FY71–72, and so on—some going all the way back to the 1930s. The older boxes were filled with brittle, yellowed claim forms. They were smudged with carbon-paper stains and freckled with typos. The signatures and countersignatures were elaborate and ornate, and Clarissa Snow imagined the signatories trying to outdo each other, engaged in inked battles of loop and filigree across the bottoms of their staid documents. She looked forward to her late-afternoon forays into the company's past, perusing the archives of a world without correction fluids and highlighters and Post-it notes, a world where—in

Clarissa Snow's rude, romantic vision—policies were never canceled and claims were never rejected. Whenever she came across a previously unexplored file box, her heart would thump. When she lifted the lid and peered inside, the dust motes of sixty years would waft up and dance around her head.

Because she received sections of the Secret Report out of sequence, Clarissa Snow was at first baffled by its contents. One section discussed the technical specifications for computer networks and telecommunications protocols. Another section consisted of pages and pages of balance sheets, the figures unlabeled. And another delineated the agenda and minutes of a business conference in Ireland. (*Ireland!* she thought, unable to imagine business being conducted in Ireland.) But one morning during Week Four—the last week of her assignment—Clarissa Snow received the opening pages of the Secret Report and discovered its secret. It was a proposal to eliminate the Claims Unit and to transfer all of its functions to an overseas vendor. In two months, the twelfth floor would become a records storage facility, and everyone in the Claims Unit would be out of a job.

Clarissa Snow snapped her eyelids shut, but it was too late. She could not unread the paragraph she had just read. She slapped at her skull with the palms of her hands, but neither hand nor fist, neither brick nor rock, could dislodge what she did not want to know. Inside the lids of her closed eyes she saw the terrain of her office multiplied a thousandfold, column after column of file boxes looming in a dense fog of gray dust.

That afternoon she locked her door and made some additional changes to the Secret Report. Using the search-and-replace function of her computer, she substituted all occurrences of the Executive Vice President's name with the word "Dickhead." Other Executive Vice Presidents became "Bunghole" and "Pedophile" and "Pig-bitch." She changed "downsizing" to "butt-fucking," "remuneration" to "masturbation," and "capital outlays" to "steaming piles of shit." She printed a copy and read it aloud. She hoped this would make her feel better. It didn't. She reversed these changes, of course, and destroyed the adulterated copy. She moved on to the file boxes. She selected one of the oldest ones—FY29–30—and poured diet soda into it, just enough to soak in and ruin the contents without seeping out. There was no relief in this, either. But Clarissa Snow—while ashamed at inflicting such petty vengeance upon these venerable and innocent artifacts—was nonetheless resolved to petty vengeance. What else could she do? *Some*body had to be punished. So she carefully poured the rest of her soda into several more boxes.

That afternoon, on her way up to the twenty-ninth floor, the Unit Manager cornered her at the elevator. "We hear tomorrow's your last day," he said. He was wearing a tie that looked like a rainbow trout, its tail fin knotted tightly beneath his chin and its head hanging wide over his belly. "You know," he said, "we're really going to miss you." Clarissa Snow's stomach churned. She thanked him.

The next day, she finished the Secret Report, assembling and formatting its sections until it was the perfect and uniform document she was hired to create. She downloaded and inserted graphics, cross-referenced an index, printed out and assembled the required number of copies, bound them into their gray report covers, and slipped them all into a box, which she was instructed to tape tightly shut and leave locked in the office along with her office key. She was done by 3:00 p.m. and was gathering her things to make her escape—the stairwell was only two doors away; no one would see her if she timed it right—when there was a knock at the door. It was the Unit Manager. "We're having a little birthday party," he told her. "And you're invited."

A banner taped to the lunchroom wall read GOODBYE CLARISSA! A cake on the table was decorated and frosted to resemble the screen of a computer terminal. The message on it read

WE'LL ALL MISS YOU! Everyone from the Claims Unit was there: the Analysts and the File Clerks, the Specialists and the Secretaries, and all the ugly-tied men. People she had never met before hugged her and handed her slices of cake and told her how *wonderful* it was having her. "We hope you come back!" they said. "We'll get you a job here!" they said. And who, who should Clarissa Snow see at this moment among the press of well-wishers but the Executive Vice President's Assistant, arising out of the crowd as if from a hole in the floor, head weaving at shoulder level—toward her—like a predatory balloon, and who, upon reaching her, executed the following in seconds: a brisk, professional hug; the cool touch of a doll-like hand upon her own; and—to Clarissa Snow's horror—an impish wink of the eye, a wink like the shutter-click of an insidious camera, a dirty little flicker of implication passed from one to the other like a pornographer's contraband. And then she was gone, slipping into the mob around the table and gliding away with a plate of cake in her hand and—to the delight of the Claims Unit employees—a creamy blue smudge of frosting on her chin. And then attention was called for—the clang of a spoon against a coffee mug—and presentations to the guest of honor were made: a bouquet of flowers, an immense tin of homemade oatmeal cookies, and, after the Unit Manager stammered through a little speech, a card signed by everyone in the Claims Unit. Clarissa Snow started to cry. Three women she didn't know cried with her.

Forty-five minutes later, in the thinning light of late afternoon, she sat hidden in her office. She was on the floor, with her knees to her chest, in a far corner of the file-box labyrinth. There were occasional knocks on the door from potential well-wishers, which Clarissa Snow ignored. She was listening for the Claims Unit stragglers to just go home, her ear attuned only to the inevitable sound of an empty office—the enormous quietudes of Friday that roll through the corridors and lap into the conference rooms and cubicles like a submerging tide. And then she could slip away, slip down the stairwell and outside and into the din and clamor of the evening exodus, leaving behind a tin of cookies that she would never taste, flowers that would be dead by Monday, and a tightly taped box heavy with Clarissa Snow's best work.

The sun was gone, and a cold wind gusted, sending trash into whirlpools on the pavement. As she walked along, Clarissa Snow set herself to the task of tearing up the going-away card. It was filled with signatures, black with names and phone numbers and congenial exhortations: "Let's do lunch!" and "Come visit!" and "Give me a call!"—forays into a world of easy acquaintance that Clarissa Snow (alas!) would never make. She tore the card into bits thoroughly and well, but left in her wake a confetti trail. It fluttered and capered behind her as she bobbed and weaved through the rush hour teem, racing for her bus. And to the momentary amusement of passersby racing for their own buses, Clarissa Snow looked like a woman in flight, like a fugitive pursued by a tiny, relentless parade that, no matter how hard she tried, she just couldn't shake.

III.

Winter came and went. Weeks of heavy rains, sheeting down concrete slopes and declivities, gushing in cataracts from gutters, sputtering from downspouts and roiling into storm drains— all of it subsided, then ceased. The sewers now sang with the rush of winter runoff, and the city, having hunkered down for the rains, seemed now to lay itself out to dry, its sidewalks steaming contentedly in the sun.

Spring was here, and progress was abloom in the Municipal Clerk's Office. A major project was under way; it was called the Conversion, and it was exactly that—the conversion of all records into a computerized database management system. Birth and death, marriage and divorce, the purchase and sale of home and property, the licensing of business entities and the bankruptcies of same—the paper trail of perfidious Fortune's sway over the lives of the inhabitants of the city would be represented as coded entries on a data field screen, tagged and cross-indexed for easy access and retrieval.

Clarissa Snow was assigned to this project, which was expected to last through the summer. The job was a plum, and Clarissa Snow—having gotten Mrs. D. out of many a job pickle—was now reaping a bounty of plums. Life in the Agency had tempered her into a loyal and hardworking employee. Her evaluations were impeccable, and her reputation was beyond reproach. She had moved into an echelon of temporary service attained by few, which conferred upon her the Agency's most coveted emblems of appreciation: the Exceptional Performance Pin and the assurance of permanent temporary employment.

Her workday in the Municipal Clerk's Office began at 8:00 a.m. This was her routine. A doughnut, an orange, and a cup of coffee at her desk accompanied her review of the contents of her in-box, which contained the previous day's Data Entry Error Run (her error stats down, always down) and the current day's Municipal Records Register Inventory. Then she was off, inventory in hand, to pull her Registers for the day. They were kept in an abandoned conference room next to the Conversion Manager's office and were stacked everywhere: on the table and the chairs, on the floor, on the wide sill along the window. Entering the dim, silent room, Clarissa Snow always felt for a moment as if she were interrupting a secret meeting. The Registers were narrow books half a yard long, with brown leather covers. Some of them had become dark and stiff and webbed with cracks, while others had been worn to a dull gold. She ran her hand over the pebbled surface of one Register, along the fissured length of another. Something stirred inside her. If she lingered, she would have imagined things about these books: that their covers, for instance, felt like maps coming to tactile life, their topographies—puckered and stubbly with age—emerging beneath her fingers; or that they looked like tiny church doors, the weathered portals to miniature cathedrals. If she lingered, she would have wondered about who filled these pages with their crabbed entries, about the lives of clerks long gone who scrivened day after day in witness to the transactions of others long gone. But Clarissa Snow did not linger. She logged out two Registers and returned to her desk.

Morning break was signaled by the appearance of the Database Systems Coordinator, who stopped by on his way to the kitchenette, his head hovering like a benevolent planet just above Clarissa Snow's cubicle partition. A twenty-second stroll to the lunchroom together, empty mugs aloft; idle chat while waiting for coffee to brew, about the Conversion—its glitches and bugs, its progress and its promise; the preparation of their coffees with creamers and sweeteners; and the return stroll to Clarissa Snow's desk, whereupon the Database Systems Coordinator, a kind and shaggy-haired bear of a man, thanked her and trudged off to his own desk. This was morning break.

She took lunch at 1:00 p.m., a late lunch to avoid the crowds. She had discovered, at the top of a multistoried parking structure, an abandoned rooftop park. There were untrimmed trees and a weed-spattered lawn. Moldy concrete benches surrounded a scummed-over pond that once contained fish. Skinny pigeons lurched about. No one else ever came here. This was her respite. Fifteen minutes to get to the park and fifteen minutes to get back to work left her with a half hour. She spread a newspaper on a bench and sat on it. She ate her bag lunch: sliced pineapple rounds, a handful of green olives, a bran cupcake, a can of vegetable juice. She closed her eyes. She listened to the rumble of cars moving beneath her and the rustle and whisper of neglected trees, still damp with rain.

She was back at work by 2:00 p.m. And upon her return every afternoon, she found sitting in the geographic center of her desktop a piece of candy, a foil-wrapped chocolate coin. (Computer monitor and keyboard were attached to an insect-like ergonomic device that suspended them in the air next to her chair. Her desktop, save for an in-box and a yellow legal pad and the day's Registers stacked neatly, was thus blissfully bare. There was no phone.) Sometimes, while settling in for the afternoon's labors, she unwrapped and ate the coin. But because chocolate held no power over her—it was merely sticky, then chalky, in her mouth, and hard to swallow—she more often than not tossed the coin into her bag and forgot about it. The mystery of the chocolate coin—Who left it? Why her?— niggled at Clarissa Snow for only the first few days of its appearance; thereafter, the regularity of its appearance on her desktop slipped easily into the regularities of her afternoon routine.

And what can be said about the rest of Clarissa Snow's afternoon? In-box: the Conversion Timeline Update and the Key Entry Rate Run (her entry rate stats up, always up). Afternoon break: nibbling on a handful of pearl onions in a far corner of the lunchroom; thumbing through a magazine, a monthly that delineated the success stories of small-business entrepreneurs; and acknowledging the halting hello of the Database Systems Coordinator, the kind and hovering largeness of him blotting out the light whenever he came upon her. Bathroom break; watercooler break; a run to the Supplies Cabinet for a fresh legal pad. And then quitting time: returning and logging her Registers and, while exiting the database and shutting down the computer, making her mental assessment of the day's work—*a good day's work,* she thought. She was delayed by chitchat with the Conversion Manager while dropping off her Register Inventory for the next day's Timeline Update, and then she was gone, zooming down the stairwell and outside to race for the 5:17 express.

She maneuvered expertly through the crowds and soon found a spot in the curbside boarding line for her bus. And as she ransacked her bag for correct change—the line was moving briskly—a shadow fell upon her and a desperate wheezing sound caused her to look up and into the stricken face of the Database Systems Coordinator. He was gasping for air. But he was also trying to speak to her, struggling with a hem and haw that—combined with his struggle for oxygen—made what he was trying to say unintelligible to Clarissa Snow. She caught something about how fast she walks, then gleaned a question of some sort, something about tomorrow's lunch hour. But she was stepping up and into the bus, and its engine was revving for departure. Impulsively, Clarissa Snow reached into the bottom of her bag and then out through the closing doors, and—by way of apology for her distraction and haste, for her inability to understand—poured into this man's massive and gentle hands a rain of coins. Gold- and silver-foiled bullion spilled around his feet as the doors shut on him and the bus roared away from the curb where he stood. Until finally he turned his head away from the receding bus, stooped heavily to pick up the litter of sweets on the pavement, and lumbered homeward, unwrapping and eating along the way each and every one of his unheeded offerings.

The 5:17 express was crammed, as usual—a stew of human heat, dank and thick and close, and Clarissa Snow loved it. She loved to ride the bus, to feel its pitch and roll beneath her feet and the vibrations of its aggrieved engine thrumming into her leg bones; to hear the swell and lull of muted conversations around her, their cadences broken by the exhilarating punch of laughter. Riding the bus, she felt immersed in the world, felt its press and push and jostle, its gentle and yielding weight sliding past and around and against her body. For this is what she loved most of all—the simple touch of another, random and intimate and essential. For no one is alone on a bus. The lowering sun flashed between high-rises, and the light that flickered in the grimy bus windows was harsh. She stood swaying blissfully against her fellow commuters and closed her eyes to the light that strobed in the windows all around her—sheets of light flipping, flipping like the pages of a dozen golden books that she would never read.

*Whoever you are! motion and reflection are especially for you,*
*The divine ship sails the divine sea for you.*
*—Walt Whitman, "A Song of the Rolling Earth"*

# Shakers

They are called P-waves. They are the primary waves, the first and the fastest, moving at up to six miles per second, near top speed through the fold and furl of basalt layer and slowing when they hit the granite massifs, the slabs of continent borne upon magmatic flows inside the earth's crust. P-waves are sound waves that move through solid rock and compress and dilate the solid rock they move through, coming at you peristaltic and slinky-like, radiating upward and outward from the seismic event. S-waves follow four to twelve seconds later, depending on where you are from the epicenter. L-waves follow soon after. These last are the slowpokes, the long-period surface waves that arrive like laggards in the seismic sequence, languid and weary, but powerful enough to do all the damage you will read and hear about when it is all over. But the P-waves come first.

When they hit, rats and snakes hightail it out of their burrows. Ants break single-file ranks and scatter blind, and flies roil off garbage bins in shimmering clouds. On the Point Reyes Peninsula, milk cows bust out of feed sheds and bolt for open pasture. Inside aquariums in dentist offices and Chinese restaurants and third-grade classrooms, fish huddle in the corners of their tanks, still as photos of huddled fish. Inside houses built on the alluvial soils of the Sacramento Delta, cockroaches swarm from behind walls, pouring like cornflakes out of kitchen cabinetry and rising in tides from beneath sinks and tubs and shower stalls. Crows go mute. Squirrels play possum. Cats awaken from naps. Dogs guilty of nothing peer guiltily at their masters. Pigeons and starlings clatter fretfully on the eaves and cornices of buildings, then rise en masse and wheel away in spectacular roller-coaster swoops. Pet-shop parakeets attempt the same maneuver in their cages. In the San Francisco Zoo, every single Adélie penguin dives and swims around and around their Plexiglas grotto, seeking the safety of what they believe to be open ocean. Big cats stop pacing, tortoises drop and tuck, elephants get antsy as pee-prone toddlers. The chimps on Monkey Island go ape-shit. Horses everywhere go mulish and nippy. Implacable cattle get skittish as deer. And a lone jogger on a fire trail on Mount Diablo gets lucky, for the starving cougar stalking her gets spooked by the subsonic pulse that rolls under its paw pads, and breaks off the hunt and heads for the hills, bounding silent and unseen up a hidden defile and leaving behind only a shudder of knotweed grass burnished amber by the waning light of an Indian summer dusk.

Subsonic pulses register in measuring devices throughout the state—in boreholes surrounding sag ponds in Big Pines and Lost Lake; in austere concrete vaults strung along abandoned railway through Donner Pass and on the peripheries of rest stops along Highway 99 through the San Joaquin Valley; and inside an array of seemingly derelict, rust-pocked, and listing corrugated-steel shacks smack in the middle of nowhere. Subsonic pulses register in instruments in firehouses, transformer substations, and the watershed property surrounding every dam in the state. In university labs and USGS offices, ink styli twitch against seismograph drums, unnoticed for now. In field stations, in Latrobe and Bear Valley and Mercey Hot Springs, the pulses are registering inside wideband seismometers, flat steel cylinders painted green and bolted onto bedrock outcrops, squat and solid as toads. In Colusa, in Cloverdale and Coalinga and Arbuckle, pulses are registering inside sleek steel-cased tubes stashed down sixty-meter boreholes. Pulses are registering in tubular, yam-size instruments embedded in grabens and scarps and streambeds in fault zones everywhere. The devices are called geophones, and their urethane casings are pumpkin orange, and there are hundreds of them pimpling vistas everywhere, from Cape Mendocino and across the geologic fretworks of the Carrizo Plain and down to the crusted shorelines of the Salton Sea, near marshes where migrating gulls think they are starfish and try to eat them.

To look at them, these field instruments—these containers embedded and tucked and stashed about—seem benign and dumb and exquisitely unperturbed. But inside them, everything is going crazy. Within precisely calibrated tolerances, tiny leaf springs recoil and pea-size bobs pendulate between capacitor plates. Feedback circuits open wide, resistors hum, and a wee electrical impulse begins a journey. Precambrian time and the making of mountains and the heat and energy that has extruded ocean floors and shoved continents apart—all is rarefied and reduced and squeezed into the gauge and extent of a titanium filament whose vibration releases a speck of data that will join the million others in a telemetric stream that, when it is all over, will tell the story of this earthquake.

Southeast of Palmdale, at a conduit box atop a phone pole along a stretch of Pearblossom Highway, a telephone lineman testing relays sways in his cherry picker. He looks down, around the perimeter of his truck thirty feet below, then at the traffic whipping past. He squints out into the desert, the horizon a laminate of browns and ochres wiggly in the heat. It is near dusk.

The air is still. He listens. And there it is again, like a wave rolling under him, and his heart skips and he lets out a hoot. His life thus far, untroubled and unremarkable—in other words, a good life—has passed without a California earthquake. He hollers: Shakers, baby! Whoo-hoo! He whirls his hips, does the tiniest of hulas in his basket high off the ground. This is never smart, but especially now—the S-waves that are following the P-waves he is dancing to will resonate with the same frequency as the vibration his hula is inducing in the hydraulic lift. When frequencies match, vibrations will increase and the hydraulic lift will shudder and lurch, and both it and the truck will keel over. The cherry picker will snap in two, and our telephone lineman will ride his basket all the way down in his first earthquake, slamming into the macadam below and the traffic streaming on it. He will be the first to die.

In the landing area of a timber tract in the Headwaters Forest, two loggers are intent on the problem of unhooking a troublesome choke line, and feel nothing. But soon the forest will keen and low, and the grinding of tree roots in the unsettled earth will grow to a deafening roar, and the loggers will drop their grapples and watch with trepidation the rumbling decks of log stacked ten feet high all around them.

A slack-jawed teen playing Grand Theft Auto in the basement of a house in San Francisco's Sunset District is too stoned to know or care whether he's winning, too stoned to remember that he's had a frozen pizza going in the microwave oven upstairs for over an hour. Yet he feels it, up through the dune sands his neighborhood was built on and through the foundation and flooring of his mother's house and through his sneakers and up deep and weird into the lengths of his shinbones.

In houseboats and fishing sleds on Shasta Lake and in sailboats bobbing in their slips along the Sausalito marina, they feel it as a series of nonrandom thumps, as if water had somehow acquired the wherewithal to come together and knock polite but resolute on the hulls of their vessels, and sounding nothing like the slap and slosh they are used to, and being disconcerting enough to give pause—beers and forks stilled halfway to expectant mouths, quesadillas and turkey patties suspended mid-flip.

Thousands give pause, hesitate, stop short. Thousands take a moment—to weigh up and sort out, to digest and to process and to see what's what. Hygienists stop flossing, butchers stop cleaving, priests stop absolving. Coupled lovers in their throes stop for just a second. Inside vehicles up and down the Nimitz and the Bayshore and strung along the Ventura and the Van Nuys, thousands of commuters cease their prattle and yammer and—abruptly compelled to ponder the Now—give pause, then speak the exact same phrase into their cell phones: Did you feel that?

A checkout clerk at end of shift in a grocery store in Watsonville feels it just as she nicks a carton of Lucky Strikes and tucks it into her backpack, and stands up and looks at everyone looking at each other. And when the shaking starts, she will hang on and watch awestruck as every single item on every single shelf leaps off in a slow-motion mass suicide and piles up three feet deep in the aisles. She will hear the great shattering of every window blowing out. And when the shaking stops, she will pick herself up and take that carton of cigarettes and step over debris and return it to its now empty shelf, and see that her hands and arms are covered with blood and embedded with broken window glass, and drop like a hammer in a dead faint.

Inmates in Folsom Prison's dining hall stop eating and glare at each other as century-old mortar shakes off the ceiling and sifts down, dusting the tops of their heads like cannoli.

In Oxnard, the local earthquake prognosticator shuffles down an alley behind Taqueria Row. A forgotten and once-ascendant surf god of the '60s—a Hurricane Nationals champ, a Duke Kahanamoku protégé—he now lives under a footbridge on the beachfront along Point Mugu, and on this day, diving dumpsters for supper, he feels—and prognosticates—nothing.

And at a vast and bustling gas station and travel center in Tracy, just off the I-205, a girl with spiky green hair climbs into a very tidy cream-colored Ford Econoline. She is nineteen but looks younger, and she is traveling light—the clothes on her back and a midsized duffel—and heading east. She tells her ride that her name is Neve, and her ride—a compact, neatly dressed man in his forties who looks older—tells her he's meeting his wife and kids in Yosemite Village. He backs the van out of its space, and as he shifts into first, his palm slips on the gear knob and he pops the clutch and kills the engine, so flustered and thrilled is he to have gotten this girl, this Neve. And before he can start the engine again, before they can be on their way, the van will begin to pitch and yaw and the cars parked around them will rise and fall as if heaved by cresting seas. Neve's ride is terrified, unable to breathe, and Neve's hand will come from nowhere and snatch his and squeeze it hard, and his hand will squeeze hers back. And for the next thirty-seven seconds they will in this fashion watch light poles and freeway signs bow deeply to one another, and watch the parking lot pavement in front of them snap and ripple, then settle like a bed-sheet. They will watch an espresso cart stagger drunk across their field of view and stagger back. They will see the treetops on hills in the distance shimmy and shake on this still and wind-less day. A chorus of car alarms will rise up around them. And when it is over, they will let go of each other and survey the damage—very little, as it happens—and they will both laugh crazily. The man will rub his hand and say: Wow, you're strong! They'll laugh some more. And then he will start up the van and ease out of the lot and onto the I-205 and take this girl where she wants to go. The radio will be on low, and they'll listen to the damage that has occurred elsewhere. They won't talk much; they won't need to, because they've been through some-thing together and that is enough. They will cross a reservoir and veer north, away from the water and into the foothills. She'll stare hard at the landscape while giving him directions, as if matching what she sees with the memory of it in her head. And just before dark she'll point to where she wants to be let off, at a busted cattle gate with the barest trace of a road behind it and nothing but arroyo and scrub all around. He'll ask her if she's sure and she'll say: Yep, this is the place. She'll get out with her duffel and thank him. We had some ride, didn't we? she'll say. And he'll say: We sure did! And he'll give her a twenty from his wallet and wish her luck and mean it. And all this he will do instead of what he was going to do to her, because of the touch of her hand, which made her human, and the fear she saw in his face that made him human like her, and that made them both the same. She will grow small and dim in his rear-view mirror, and when she waves, he'll wave back. And as he returns to the travel center in Tracy to get another girl, he'll wonder what will become of this girl—this Neve—out here, in the middle of nowhere.

The middle of nowhere. In Death Valley, a string of ultra-marathoners on mile sixty-five of a hundred-mile course weaves along sticky blacktop road in 115-degree heat, sucking hard at unyielding air and trailed by ESPN news crews in satellite vans. Miles from nowhere in Sierra Nevada high country, on a mudflat of lake bed sun-baked hard and gray as pavement, hundreds camp out for a motocross rally. Somewhere along a desolate stretch of sea cliff due west of the Coast Highway, through cypress and thickets of scrub oak, then over the edge and seventy-five feet straight down and under cold black water, divers feel along cleft and crag with numbed fingers, poaching abalone. Deep inside the old-growth woods of Plumas or Lassen or Kings Canyon—regions so remote that rangers have yet to map or break trail therein—pot farmers dangle fishhooks at eye level around their crops, and a meth cooker crazy from isolation and from paint thinner and acetone fumes sets punji stakes inside pits dug around his makeshift lab. On a map, the roads end in the Granite Mountains north of the Mojave. Dotted lines, then white space—nothing. But in the Granite Mountains, air force personnel in air-conditioned Nissen huts play foosball, microwave corn dogs, and watch Oprah on TV. In terrains unreachable by road or trail, mountain bikers whoop and tear up and down the broken, rain-rutted slopes of hidden gullies, and hang gliders pitch off bluffs, wheeling high above tiny golden fans of virgin beach and an ocean inflamed by the sun dropping into it. In the middle of nowhere, phone company technicians rappel down slopes and hack through Douglas fir and sugar pine to erect cell towers disguised as Douglas fir and sugar pine. And in Joshua Tree National Park, a day hiker off trail in the Pinto Mountains lies at the bottom of a ravine with a broken left ankle and a mangled right knee. He lies prone and still to avoid the grinding pain when he moves either leg. His water bottle is empty. His cell phone is gone, lost on the craggy slopes above him—his cigarettes are somewhere up there, too, and his sunglasses—and he has no warm clothing for the cold desert night coming on. He is hoarse and thirsty, and feeling humbled and stupid, and wondering whether he really could die out here, just three miles from his car parked in the lot of a gift shop that sells trail maps and nature guides and bottled water and sunglasses and tote bags and key chains and postcards—HOTTER'N HELL IN JOSHUA TREE! WISH YOU WERE HERE!

It is like this here: Get off the interstate, get anywhere off of it and drive away, onto State Route 16 to Gold Country, or Route 36 into Trinity Wilderness, or 178 toward the Piutes. Find a smaller road and take it, then a smaller road, and take that—the one that squiggles like a heartbeat's trace along a skinny ridge; the one that winds through an endless wold of identical hummocks; the road cut that is barely road or cut, cinched tight across the midsection of sheer mountain wall; or the straightaway that shoots into the empty flats below you and fades into the distant haze, becoming more an erasure of a road than a road itself. Keep going. Go past signs with the names of towns on them that make you chuckle: Peanut and Fiddletown and Raisin City, Three Rocks and Copperopolis, Look Out and Rescue and Honeydew. Listen to the static on your radio, which picks up nothing here in the middle of nowhere. Marvel at how fucking big this state is. Allow yourself to be seduced by notions of vastness and desolation. Do this, and a pickup truck crammed with paint cans and ladders, or bundles of steel pipe or a dining-room set, will rise up and loom in your mirrors and rattle past you like the clamorous armies of Death himself, late for the Apocalypse. Do this, and in the middle of boundless farmland devoid of human landmark to all horizons, you will come across a sprinkler going. On the shoulders of derelict roads you will see mailboxes huddled like abandoned old men, weathered and stooped, and among them, today's paper inside a bright blue tube. Around a curve that brings into view an unbroken panorama of brown mesas and buttes, you will see graffiti, bold and crass, painted high on a rock face: baroque gang tags or cryptic acronyms, or GO TITANS! or I LOVE YOU VANESSA! Chained to a lone dead tree you will see a lidless rust-chancred garbage can—forsaken, forlorn, God's Last Garbage Can—filled with fresh, logoed trash from Taco Bell and Hardee's. At sunset, the spectacular scenery that you've begun to ignore will recede into shadows, into night, until you are hurtling through a tube of darkness. In the wedge of your headlights the road sweeps under you, and there is only the ember glow of the dashboard, and the thump and thrum of the tires, and the static on the radio turned low and hissing steady like a whisper of distant rain. And just when you succumb once again to the romance of solitude, you see lights up ahead. You tap your brakes, and this is what glides past you—a neat little cottage with a fence and a lawn, the porch light a fever of beetles and moths; in the windows, the water of light from a TV; from the chimney, a steady white finger of smoke; and in the gravel driveway, a freshly washed car, beaded and gleaming. And then it is gone, sailing into the night, and for a moment you're not sure you saw what you saw. But there it is, glimmering small and bright in your rearview mirror for a long time, until it finally drops into a dip of road behind you. And you realize you couldn't get lost here if you tried. And you've tried. The middle of nowhere is always somewhere for somebody.

Down a densely wooded gorge in the Siskiyou Mountains, the bones of a hiker lie scattered in the underbrush, long picked clean by coyotes and crows and grown brown and mossy in the cool dirt. Inside the mud at the bottom of the San Francisco Bay, hundreds of commuters rustle and sway on trains rattling through the Transbay Tube. In a ninth-floor dorm room on the UCLA campus, two students who've just tearfully broken up have breakup sex on a futon in the corner. One room over, a young woman gingerly presses her entire body against the wall to listen, rapt as an acolyte apprehending the mystery of the divine. And four floors down, an unfinished letter to Mom sits atop the rubble of a desk. Its last line is: I hate it here. And its author is cross-legged on the floor, tearing the pages from hundred-dollar engineering textbooks and gazing as if sun blind into a floodlit vision of disappointment and ruin.

In an efficiency studio high up a tower block in Bakersfield, or in an upscale-ish condo on the fringes of a dicey neighborhood in Inglewood, or in an in-law unit wedged beneath a house that clings to the Oakland Hills, or in a loft or duplex or railroad flat in Rio Linda or Citrus Heights or Gilroy, you are watching TV.

You are sitting in a leather club chair in the middle of an otherwise spare room. You are home early from the office, having feigned a headache worse than the one you really do have. You are drinking a beer, watching the local news anchor read. Her name is Wendy Something, and you have a crush on her. You moved here only months ago—from Cedar Falls, from Monroe or Meridian, from Canton, Grand Forks, Eau Claire—and you have yet to make friends. The weekly drink with coworkers has drifted into a less occasional gathering, then none at all, as you've gradually discovered you have little in common, and you get along well at work anyway, so why even bother?

People are hard to get to know out here, inside their bubbles, with their benign, almost tender indifference toward you and their studious gestures of intimacy—the banter that is devoid of subtext and the How-are-you! that is never a question and the See-you-later! that simply signals the end of conversation. It has been lonely. You come home in the evenings and eat a take-out burrito over the kitchen sink and stroll through your half-furnished rooms, with books in alphabetized stacks on the floor and unpacked boxes as end tables and nothing on the walls. You have pondered this metaphor for an unfinished life—or better, the beginning of a new one—and you remind yourself why you moved here, why everyone moves here. And you may be lonely like this forever, but out here at least it *feels* transitory— a step on a journey, a blip on a timeline, and all that.

Joists groan overhead. A window frame stutters in its casement and is shot open. A kitchen chair is scraped across a floor. Movement above you. The sound of other people.

The sun will set within the hour. It is a time of day you love, between the room growing dark and you turning the lights on.

They crow about their light out here. In the early twentieth century, artists came in droves to paint in California light, adjusting color schemes and developing a choppy brushstroke and applying the paint quickly so as to capture on canvas the fleeting quality of the light—the "temporal fragment," the "instantaneous view." Out here they go on about how the light chisels, how it polishes and defines the edges of whatever it falls upon and imparts a dazzling clarity. They go on about how the light comes down around you in curtains or how it pours and spills like honey. It gleams and glints, it sparks and flares. The light has weight, it has density, it is palpable. Sometimes you can even hear it, zinging metallic and bright! What crap. When they aren't steeped in the clichéd golden hues of a shampoo commercial, the skies most days are an insipid palette of white and bluish white and yellowish white. Every vista is dull and bleary, a sun-bleached smudge in the distance. And nothing is chiseled.

Everything you look at is foreshortened, flat and common as a souvenir poster. Although there can be days—those mornings of unseasonable fog when the sunlight is filtered through a fragile veil of cloud that renders the air itself luminous as milk; or the clear, cloudless afternoon when you're walking under a canopy of trees or through the lobby of a building downtown, and just before moving out of the shade, you take off your sunglasses and stand there a moment and anticipate entering the world of sunlight.

You take a swig of beer. You catch the whiff of a cigarette— the woman above you, smoking out of her window. You've said hello to her. She's said hello back.

On the TV, something is up with Wendy Something. She stops mid-sentence and looks off camera. You feel a bump beneath you, then another. The ceiling joists begin to groan loud and steady, and all your windows are rattling like maracas. Wendy is hanging on to her bucking desk, that on-air equanimity of hers that you love pretty much gone. She is looking right at you, and then the screen goes to snow and the TV tips over. There is a pounding like the fists of giants against the building you live in. There is a muffled cry from the woman above you, and you finally apprehend what is happening. You take a breath, chug your beer, toss the empty bottle over your shoulder. You hang on tight to your fat, heavy chocolate leather chair—your gift to yourself for finally making the move out here. You hang on and you think: *The shaking will either stop or keep going. Life is lived from moment to moment.*

On a grassy knoll overlooking an ocean view in Pacific Grove, two lovers on a blanket sip wine from plastic cups, reveling in a silence between them that goes on and on. A rice farmer, shin-high in flooded fields, stops brooding over weed infestation and a late harvest to watch the sunlight shatter and reshatter on the surface of the waters. A tiny old woman seated on a crowded bus barreling along an express lane peels a tangerine with the gravity and precision of bomb disposal. A grill cook on break from a hellish workday lolls on a bed of flattened boxes in an alley, and with absolutely nothing on his mind—hellish day gone!—watches a queue of mare-tailed clouds file across a slot of sky high above him.

A Riverside County sheriff loops through the parking lot of the Oasis Visitor Center in Joshua Tree National Park. The center is closed, and the lot is empty except for a silver Honda hatchback. His last stop before going off shift, the sheriff idles in the middle of the lot inside his beautiful new-issue Chevy Tahoe. The sun moves behind a row of fan palms, their long shadows reaching for him. It is windless and still. He lingers in this anticipatory moment, then punches the gas and cranks the wheel and hangs on, going around and around, reduced to breathlessness and gooseflesh from the thunder of 240 horses in his bones and the delicious centrifugal tug on his innards and the darkling hills and mustard skies of a desert dusk streaking and smearing all tilt-a-whirl around his head.

Three miles to the southeast, the owner of a forgotten Honda hatchback lies at the bottom of a ravine. He is very thirsty. His skin is sunburn pink. A line of shadow slices his body in two, and in the shaded half it's cold already. His ankle swells inside a boot he can't reach to untie and take off, and his right knee is big as a cantaloupe and awful to look at. Plus there's something wrong with his elbow; he can't move his arm. All in all, a shitty day. And then the earth begins to move. The rock debris in the talus he is lying in shimmies and shudders and shoves him around. Scree chatters down the slopes of the ravine. He is pelted with stones and submerged in a cloud of desert dust. The quake subsides, the cloud settles. His eyes are cut and raw from grit, and his mouth is filled with sand. He hacks and coughs, igniting his legs with pain, and his heaving soon gives way to sobs. He is desolate and alone. He is so dehydrated that tears do not come.

And hours from now, after the sun has gone down, when he is shivering from the cold, when the cold is all he can think about, something remarkable will happen. A diamondback rattlesnake will home in on his heat trace and unwind itself from the mesh of a creosote bush and drop to the ground and seek the warmth of his body against the chill evening, slicing through the sand and sweeping imperiously between his legs and turning into itself until coiled tight against his groin and draped along his belly with the offhand intimacy of a lover's arm. He will watch its dumpling-size head in repose on his sternum go up and down with his breathing, its eyes open and indifferent and exquisitely wrought—tiny bronzed beads stippled black and verdigris. And his breaths will soon come slow and steady, and his despair will give way to something wholly unexpected. He is eyeball to eyeball with a rattlesnake in the powdery moonglow of the Mojave Desert. He can hear birds calling back and forth—birdsong!—in the middle of nowhere. He can look up at a night sky that is like gaping into a chasm boiling with stars, as if the celestial spigots were opened wide and jammed, and he can remember nothing of the life he's lived up to now. And he will shake, not from cold nor fear, nor from any movements of the earth, but from some vague and elemental conviction about wholeness or harmony or immortality. He will shake, resolute in a belief in the exaltation of this moment, yet careful not to disturb the lethal snake on his chest. *How cool is this!* he will think. *Wish you were here!* he will think.

# Acknowledgments

This book has been a long time coming and a lot of people helped. Thank you, all. Thanks for waiting.

Mitzi Angel
Sarah Burnes
Eli Horowitz, M.M.M. Hayes, and Ben George
The MacDowell Colony, the National Endowment for the Arts, the Lannan Foundation, and the Idaho Commission on the Arts
Robert Wrigley and Kim Barnes
Susan Hutton and Michael Byers
Ann Joslin Williams, Angela Pneuman, Jacob Molyneux, Malinda McCollum, Andrea Bewick, and Bay Anapol
Tobias Wolff, Elizabeth Tallent, Gilbert Sorrentino, and John L'Heureux

Janet Silver, Lois Rosenthal, and Will Allison
Maya Sonenberg, David Shields, Lauro Flores, and David Bos-
    worth
Molly Giles and Michelle Carter
Lionel Ivan Orozco

A NOTE ABOUT THE AUTHOR

Daniel Orozco's stories have appeared in *Best American Short Stories*, *Best American Mystery Stories*, *Best American Essays*, and the *Pushcart Prize Anthology*, as well as in publications such as *Harper's Magazine*, *Zoetrope: All-Story*, *McSweeney's*, *Ecotone*, and *StoryQuarterly*. He was awarded a 2006 NEA Fellowship and was a finalist for a 2006 National Magazine Award. He teaches in the Creative Writing Program at the University of Idaho.